GADGET MAN

GADGET MAN

RON GOULART

WILDSIDE PRESS

GADGET MAN

Published by:
Wildside Press
P.O. Box 301
Holicong, PA 18928
www.wildsidepress.com

FIRST WILDSIDE PRESS EDITION:
JULY 2001

GADGET MAN

CHAPTER 1

The mad girl flashed angily across the bright tower room and interfered with the view of the riot. Two plainclothes therapists dived into the big circular room on her trail, apologetic, and hunkered so as to leave the tinted windows clear for watching. The girl, thin and fair, shrugged out of the reach of the lead therapist and ran straight at Sergeant James Xavier Hecker. He was already up out of his vinyl wing chair, reaching one calming hand to her. "Just be easy now," he said.

In the chair next to his, Therapist-in-Chief Weeman said, "Halt, Mrs. Gibbons." He stretched over and slapped the slim girl with his clip-on stunrod. She stiffened just short of touching Hecker.

"Why that?" asked Hecker, steadying the girl's now paralyzed body.

"We strive to give our more hopeful patients a semblance of autonomy and free motion," said Weeman. He

1

breast-pocketed the stunrod in his lime-green tunic. "In-cidents can't be encouraged, but on the other side of the token, neither should they be subdued with too drastic means."

The two therapists hesitated, hands extending, unob-trusively, for the caught patient. Hecker said, "It'll take her two hours to come out of that." He let the two wide men carry the girl away and out of the top tower of the Rehab Center.

Weeman tugged at his blond beard, as though he sud-denly suspected it was false. "I find your concern for a disturbed suburban housewife, a girl you don't even know, to be almost fascinating."

"Why don't you turn those Kendry files over, and I'll take off." Hecker was a lean man, tall and slightly bent, with a bony face and too big hands. The Social Wing of the Police Corps had allowed him to grow a shaggy mus-tache, but would probably not promote him much beyond sergeant.

Therapist-in-Chief Weeman's small, tidy lap was filled with carded microfilm. He let some of the fingers of his left hand dance on the film and nodded at the view win-dows. "I wish you shared my fascination with these riots, though your reasons for not doing so are best known to yourself. That one occurring down there in Citrus Knolls right now seems rich in fascination. I've monitored all the recent suburban riots in the area, but this is the first one to take place in, as you might say, my own back yard."

Far below and across an artificial river, a troop of cub scouts had just put torches to the community recreation center, and to the immediate left of that a mob of graying matrons were lobbing plastic bombs into the main building of the tennis club. The majority of the members of the Veterans of the Chinese Invasion were chucking surplus grenades into patios and rock gardens all along Citrus Knolls's wide and neatly pastoral streets and lanes. Over two thousand of the residents of the planned suburb, a good third of its population, were involved in the rioting and looting. "Here come the troops," said Hecker, turning his back on the windows.

Weeman toggled a switch on his chair arm, and television screens on the blind wall of the rehabilitation center tower snapped alive. "I want a better look at all this. These initial confrontations between the dazed citizens and the Army of the Republic of Southern California are little less than fascinating."

Hecker glanced up at the images of the lime-and-lemon-uniformed Republic of Southern California soldiers marching with locked arms down the main esplanade of Citrus Knolls. "The Kendry files," he repeated.

"What do you, as a representative of the Social Wing, a division of our Southern California government I can't help believing is more liberal than necessary, think causes these outbreaks in our best suburbs, Sergeant?" Weeman twisted new curls into his full beard, ticked his head forward. The army was apparently using stun gas, and the screen showed people slowing and freezing, still clutching torches and bombs and bright new rifles.

"The riots are the Junta's business," said Hecker. "They govern the Republic of Southern California."

"You seem reluctant to express an opinion that is solidly yours, Sergeant Hecker."

"I just work here."

"Look at that," said Weeman. "That little old lady sniped one of the cameramen off the roof of the United

3

Methodist." He studied then the microfilm between his legs, watched Hecker for several long seconds. "Some people, a small but vocal minority, consider the cause of the riots to be the recent tightening of law enforcement and the additional troops being garrisoned in some of our larger secured towns and cities. What do you, Sergeant Hecker, feel about the notion that the Junta has ruled the Republic with undue strictness in recent years?"

"Since my branch of the Police Corps is under the jurisdiction of the Junta, you don't have to ask," Hecker told him. He paced away from the seated therapist, watching, briefly, the smoke columns fuse into a thick black smear in the bright afternoon sky.

"Younger people," said Weeman, "forget how things were back in nineteen eighty-one and those years. Before the Chinese Commandos were defeated in the Battle of Glendale, there were many, not deluded but calm and rational people, who felt Red China would successfully carry off its land invasion of Southern California."

"If Southern California hadn't seceded from the Union in nineteen-eighty, things wouldn't have happened as they did."

"The President of the United States, even though his country was falling apart, should have supported us," said Weeman. "Had the Junta not been formed, merging our best Southern California military and industrial brainpower into one dedicated and loyal ruling think tank, there would have been black days for the Republic. You, a man in his middle or late twenties, don't remember those bad times."

"Probably not." Hecker returned and sat next to the Therapist-in-Chief. "I have a contact point to be at by tonight."

4

"This has been, thanks to younger residents of the Republic such as yourself, Sergeant Hecker, rightly christened the 'Age of Anxiety.'" Weeman twined his stubby fingers in the swatch of beard beneath his chin. "Myself, Sergeant Hecker, I favor the conspiracy theory to explain the riots. These most recent suburban riots—there's a strange and fascinating quality to them." He freed his fingers from his facial hair and indicated the burning and fighting below. "Social repressions, supposed injustices and unlawful restraints, don't invoke the kind of mania we're witnessing at this moment, Sergeant Hecker. A thoughtful examination of the sweeping panorama of riot history tells us that citizens in comfortable one-hundred-thousand-dollar homes in landscaped and secured areas should not loot and burn. They're not blacks, are they, most of them?" He bundled the microfilm cards and tossed them across to Hecker. "The classic riots in the United States and, especially because of our near-tropic climate, in Southern California, have traditionally been the work of militant black men, Sergeant Hecker. And sometimes the fiery Mexican-American. Though you may not be aware, at this remote place in time, of that."

"We studied those riots in school," said Hecker. He thumbed through the cards, holding them next up to the overhead lights in turn. "Most of this information on the Kendry family we have in our Social Wing files. I thought you had some extra stuff that couldn't be trusted to transmission."

Weeman drew a last card from beneath his narrow thigh. "Some background material on Jane Kendry. Tests and projections done during the brief period when she was a ward of the Rehab system. What exactly is your mission for SW, Sergeant?"

Hecker took the new card in one big-knuckled hand, walked to a wall microfilm reader and inserted the card. "You were told that when the Social Wing requested this interview."

"That story wasn't a cover then? Somebody in the Kendry clan has sent the Social Wing word that they have information on the cause of the riots?"

"The nature of the information sent and the procedures suggested tend to indicate the Kendry family or some of their followers may be involved," Hecker said. The young face of a lean, intense girl rolled into view on the screen of the reader. She had smooth, tan skin, hair of a red-gold color, long. "Jane Kendry," muttered Hecker to himself.

"Seven years ago," said Weeman. "She was fifteen then, coltish. Her wild father and a bunch of the clan broke her out of a minimum-security Rehab Center down near the Laguna Sector. Lovely marine view there. She's a quirky girl, and I believe that it is Jane Kendry who runs that band of guerrillas, that growing band of guerrillas. Her father, old Jess, is in his middle sixties now, ridden with addictions and badly healed wounds. At first the guerrillas were all Kendry family, but in recent years the ranks have been swollen with other types of dissidents and anarchists. Jane is a tough girl, Sergeant Hecker, and you won't find that hopeful look the picture there shows us. Not any more with Jane Kendry. Is she your contact?"

"I don't know," said Hecker. "Our information isn't that specific. We have a contact point fairly close to one of the unsecured towns the Kendrys are thought to sometimes operate in. There's a safe-conduct pass of sorts. I came here to fill myself in on the Kendrys more thoroughly."

6

Therapist-in-Chief Weeman rose up behind Hecker. "You look quite unlike a policeman, even a Social Wing one, in your civilian clothes." He flickered a sequence of toggles and the view windows blanked, the monitor screens died. "Listen to me now, Sergeant Hecker. I worked on the Kendry girl's case down there in Laguna Sector seven years ago. I liked her and felt I was reaching her. We could work together on her problems and conflicts. Then those wild men came in and smashed things and wrenched her away."

Hecker stopped reading the micro file. "So?"

"I have authority to bring her in for rehabilitation," he said, moving closer to the Social Wing sergeant. "If she wishes, we can help her. Fit her back into the legitimate processes of the Republic of Southern California. She's a girl with fascinating potential."

"She may not want back in. Her exile is probably voluntary."

"We often think that, Sergeant, and we are often wrong," said the therapist. "If you see Jane Kendry, offer. Tell her Therapist-in-Chief—No, she knew me as Associate Therapist and without the beard, younger—tell her Dr. Weeman can get her safe conduct here to the Pasadena Rehab Center. It could be her only chance."

Hecker frowned. "Wait now. Why her only chance?"

"You may, Sergeant Hecker, have some competition in your quest for Jane Kendry."

"And I may not even see her," he said. "But who else is searching for her?"

"Are you familiar with Second Lieutenant Same?"

"Norman Same? He's with the Manipulation Council. Why do they want Jane Kendry?"

"Why does Manipulation usually want people?" said

7

the therapist. "The Junta must have locked her away or —forgive the dark thought—simply killed her. The guerrillas are trouble, and Second Lieutenant Same, who has been here too, seeking background material, believes Jane Kendry leads the guerrillas."

"Maybe there's been a leak in the Social Wing, if Same has been here already." Hecker clicked his bony thumb against his teeth. "We'll see, then."

"You get to her and tell her to be careful," said Weeman. "Once she's here in Rehab I can guarantee they won't touch her. Believe me, Sergeant Hecker, when I tell you I can really help Jane Kendry."

"I'll tell her," said Hecker. "Now I'll retrieve my hopper from your roof port and get on."

On the highest roof of the five-towered Rehab Center, Hecker could see Citrus Knolls burning away, blackening the day. His unmarked Social Wing hopper was not in the reserved slot of the rooftop landing area. Two orange-uniformed soldiers of the RSC Army were squatting where the small heliplane had been.

"Looking for your machine?" asked one of the soldiers, bouncing inquisitively and making his buttocks smack the topping lightly.

"Yes, indeed," said Hecker. He, being in civilian clothes, had his blaster pistol cupped under his arm and not quickly accessible. "You boys take it?"

"Sorry, Sarge," said the other soldier. They were both young privates. "We needed extra wings, and the order went out. Your Social Wing reported an unmarked hopper parked here, signed out to Sergeant James Xavier Hecker, and it was picked up. They got your hopper over to Citrus Knolls, using it to dust stun powder on the folks trying to dismantle the shopping plaza."

Hecker surveyed the roof. There was a pitted old surplus hopper, with the ARSC insignia still vaguely visible on its side, parked nearby. "Who does that one belong to?"

"That's for you if you want to use it," said the bouncing private. "Corporal Bozes said you could use it. That's why we hung around—to be helpful. That clunk isn't much for altitude, and there's not enough armor on its belly. Those humping snipers can set your tail on fire easy enough as it is, without flying over in a thing like that."

"I hope it'll do for me," said Hecker. "I have an appointment."

"Plenty good for Social Wing purposes," said the private and bounced again.

In five minutes Hecker was in the air. He had to be in San Emanuel Sector, a beach town beyond the Laguna Sector, by nightfall. The town was not one the military rated as secured, and he could expect no help from any officials of the RSC or the Police Corps once he got there. The old army hopper, which he'd have to ditch before he got in sight of San Emanuel, chugged through the sky. It strained for altitude, whining, for nearly a half hour, then began making rumbling, pocking sounds and dropped from the sky toward a stretch of scrubby beach. Hecker's safety straps snapped as he tried to right the ship. When the crash came, he was slammed hard into the control panel.

CHAPTER 2

The hopper was moving away from him in pieces, like a jigsaw puzzle dissolving. There were weathered, gritty hands all around him and raw smells of the sea and strong spices. Gray clothes and close-cropped hair. Hecker caught at himself and sat back. Hands were sliding through his clothes, and one hand snapped out his packet of identification material, another got his pistol. Since he'd passed into Rehab Center on retinal and voice prints, the packet contained only the faked papers he was to use on his trip into the unsecured towns. Plus the dog-eared business card with the drawing of a gull on it, the one which had come into Social Wing headquarters with the message from the possible Kendry contact.

Hands had found the card and someone said, "Kendry pass. Leave him safe and alive."

Hecker's pistol was returned, tucked back into its pouch and patted. "Scavengers," he said, seeing a little better.

"Beach people." The old army hopper was dismantled completely, and its pilot seat, still holding Hecker, was tipped in a clump of beach scrub. The sky had thinned and the wind had grown warm. It was late in the afternoon now, and when Hecker touched at his head he found a swelling spreading across the left side of his face, a smear of dry blood in its center.

The man with his hands still on Hecker was old, sixty-five or more, and dry with age and sun. "Want to talk, you can talk. Want to eat, you can eat. Want to hide, you can hide. I'm Rius." He seemed to have too many ribs. They lined his thin body in places where there shouldn't be ribs. "The military won't venture into this stretch. You find yourself in the Manhattan Beach Sector, south of Venice."

"I've got to," said Hecker, letting Rius help him to stand, "get to San Emanuel by tonight."

"He does know the Kendrys," said a tall, blonde girl. She was wearing a pair of thin gray shorts and mismatched souvenir moccasins.

"We're free and easy here," Rius told him. He had a plastic bag of green chili peppers in the pocket of his shorts. "He doesn't have to talk. Or share."

"I seem to have already shared my hopper with you," said Hecker. He found he could walk and took himself clear of the grasp of the old man.

"Rights of salvage," said Rius. "An ancient law of the sea." He bit a pepper in half and pointed with the uneaten portion at the Pacific Ocean.

The glare of the sun on the water made Hecker turn away. Along the beach were scattered fifty people, most of them dressed as simply as Rius and the blonde. Hecker stretched out a long, lanky arm and took his identification folder from Rius, along with the Kendry card. "Much obliged."

"Would you," asked the blonde, "like to talk about your problems? Are you thinking of quitting the formal culture up there in the Republic?"

"He's free to talk or not to talk," reminded Rius, starting another chili pepper. "That's the way we are here."

"If you'd like to talk about what business you have with the Kendrys," said the tall blonde, who had small breasts, "you can do that, too."

A plump, pale man with his hair recently cropped padded over the sand and squinted at Hecker. "They didn't mention you till now. I'm Dr. Jay V. Leavitt. What happened? Oh, no, that's right . . . you don't have to tell me. That's how it is here."

"My hopper crashed, and then you guys dismantled it for scrap," said Hecker. "I'll talk freely about that. My head hit the instrument panel in the crash because the safety belts snapped."

"I bet nobody even asked you how you came by that old army hopper," said the doctor.

"I borrowed it."

The doctor smiled and shrugged. "My wife lets me spend a month down here each spring. May I feel your head?"

"Sure."

"We live in a condominium in Pacific Palisades. It's our second condominium. The first one we owned fell into the ocean. But I don't have to worry about things like that here." He poked his sandy fingers at Hecker's swollen face. "I'm not even sterile. I hope it won't cause an infection."

"Don't worry yourself."

13

"No brain damage, I guess." The doctor thumbed down Hecker's lower eyelids. Then rapped his head. "And no sign of a fracture. I bet you don't even have much of a concussion. You could rest up here on the beach a couple of days if you like, though I'm not prescribing. The nights get cold but we build fires."

"I'm en route to San Emanuel."

"You should talk to Marsloff and Percher," Dr. Leavitt told him. He screwed his forefinger around in the pocket of his new gray shorts. "I had some Band-Aids in here. No, all used up."

"Who are Marsloff and Percher?"

"Drive one of the land trucks," said the blonde girl. "They're going to try to get down to the San Diego Sector tonight with a load of salvage. Dr. Leavitt is probably suggesting you could catch a ride as far as San Emanuel with them. If he doesn't mind my speaking for him."

"Not at all," replied the doctor. "You're a very bright girl. Were you possibly a receptionist or dental-hygiene nurse up in the Republic?"

"Only a housewife," said the blonde. "I could never have any satisfactory conversations with my husband. He's in riot-control research and used to bring new equipment home to try out." To Hecker she said, "You have to be a little careful of Percher. He's a gadget freak."

"Oh," said Hecker. He'd worked with gadget cases in the Social Wing.

"A gadget freak is a person," explained Dr. Leavitt, "who uses machines and appliances in unnatural ways to produce electric brain stimulation and other potentially dangerous, though momentarily pleasurable, effects. Unlicensed electric brain stimulation was outlawed well over two years ago by the Junta."

14

"Where's his partner, this Marsloff?" asked Hecker.

"They're both of them off down there." The blonde indicated the location with a turn of her head. "See the old fallen-down beach restaurant that says POOR BOY on its side. Their truck is hidden in there. Marsloff is the big and dark-haired man leaning on the rail. Percher's a little blond fellow. He's in their truck probably."

"He rewired an electric mixer to stimulate himself with last night," said the doctor sadly. "A bright young man otherwise, when he's not comatose."

"You should have been here when he got inside a re-built soft-drink machine," said the blonde. "Want me to walk over with you?"

"Sure," said Hecker. She started down the sand, and he moved in beside her. "Been out here long?"

"A year, I guess. My name's Hildy. You don't have to tell me yours. We don't care here."

"James Xavier Hecker." His fake papers had used his real name.

"I read your ID packet. 'Jim' do they call you?"

"'Hecker' usually," said Hecker.

"Hey, Marsloff. Rius says it's okay if you help this guy." She stopped a few yards from the big man. "He knows the Kendrys. He wants a lift south."

Marsloff strode over. He had gray-black hair, short on his head and long and swirling on most of his body. "Can you drive a truck?"

"Yes."

"My partner, Percher, is a gadget freak. He found half a dozen old-fashioned electric toothbrushes this morning, and he's knocked himself blooey again in the cab of our truck. Has his own portable generator back in what used

15

to be the pantry of the café. He's in a coma right this minute."

"Shouldn't you get Leavitt to look at him?"

"This isn't the Republic," said Marsloff. "He always comes out of it. He doesn't favor anybody tinkering with him when he's having one of his comas. I'll leave him here in the shack, under a quilt, for this haul. You watch him a little, Hildy?"

"If you like."

Marsloff studied the westering sun. "We'll leave in a half hour. How far south?"

"San Emanuel," said Hecker. The sunlight wasn't bothering him as much now.

"You do know the Kendrys, then." Marsloff grinned. "Percher smuggled in some beer from the Tijuana Enclave, real Mexican beer. It's warm because he's been using the ice machine on himself. Wait here and I'll get us a couple bottles. We can cool them off in the ocean." He patted Hecker and the girl on their backs and climbed over fallen wood and plaster into the remnants of the seashore café.

CHAPTER 3

The hanging sign that caught the night wind said GIA-
COMO OF SAN EMANUEL on it. The sign flapped over the
doorway of a building that was gone. There were only
traces of a collapsed wharf out this close to the ocean
now, fragments of restaurants and shops. It was his contact point, and Hecker stood there on a firm section of
wharf, hearing nothing except the dark water moving
across the cluttered sand below the pilings. There were
mounds of seashells dotting this section of San Emanuel
beach, twists of dead seaweed. The wind carried what
looked like a tatter of red-checkered tablecloth up above
Hecker's head, and the cloth fought and twisted, fluttering free and fading into the darkness among the fallen
timbers and planking. He thought of the girl who had
tried to reach him in the Rehabilitation Tower.

"See the card. Let's see the card," said a boy's voice.

Hecker carefully turned. "What card?"

The boy was too small for his age. He seemed to be
about fifteen and was barely five feet tall. His legs were
thin and subtly twisted, and his arms were thin, too, and
bent in wrong ways. He was holding a big shaggy cat
in his arms, close to his bare chest. "I'm a younger
brother," he told Hecker. "An adopted brother, actually.
I'm Kendry, though." The cat was limp but awake. It
lolled comfortably, watching Hecker with its round
yellow-green eyes.

"Tell me the cat's name," said Hecker.

"Burrwick," the boy said, "if you have to have the coun-
tersign crap. Now let's see the card. Fetch it out slowly
or you'll feel some steel in your fat ribs."

"I look fat to you?" Hecker drew out the ID packet,
located the card with the gull drawn on it in pale-blue
writing fluid.

The boy took the card, held it near his face. "Everybody
seems fat. I hid from the soldiers too long, missed out
on too many meals. They call that malnutrition, you
know, all that business with vitamins and minerals. I read
up on it all but haven't been able to change myself much
so far."

"Don't be discouraged," said Hecker. "It takes patience.
Can you tell me who sent you to meet me?"

"Not allowed to." The cat mewed once, tapped on the
boy's narrow chest. "I'm to guide you to a conclave. A
family gathering mostly, a Kendry thing. Be hundreds
there, Kendrys and other of the guerrillas. Though some
of the real good underground fighters don't go for these
kind of festivities. Guerrillas grew out of the Kendry clan.
Kendrys been pouring into this part of California since
long time before everything fell apart. You're to palm
yourself off as a cousin by marriage to old Mace Kendry.

18

Use your real name, or whatever name you're traveling under. You married Mace's second oldest daughter, Reesie. They were both ridden down by the RSC Army, are dead now. You been in a solitary cell down in San Pedro Sector since shortly after you got married two years ago. You were let out on the Junta's last birthday amnesty two years ago. You got this card—here, take it back —from Mace one time, and you heard about tonight's gathering in a bar in Venice named Uncle Avram's. Can you remember all this crap?"

"Most of it."

"Better get it all straight. Mace, in case somebody asks, had his left arm missing from just below the elbow due to a Police Corps blaster. Reesie was a tall girl, big-boned with bad front teeth. Okay-looking, but too meaty." The boy rubbed the cat's stomach. "With a couple hundred at least Kendrys together, there's likely to be some want to kill you for the sport. If you give them the added inspiration of lying and stumbling in your yarn, you'll surely feel steel from several directions."

"Thanks," said Hecker. "What's your name?"

"It isn't part of the password crap." The boy beckoned Hecker to follow him.

Walking away from the fallen wharf, Hecker said, "I wanted to know just for myself."

"Jack," said the boy.

"Jack."

"Know where I got that name?"

"No." They turned onto a street that wound between still-standing but long-vacant shops and hotels. The municipal trees had grown wild, and there was a thick tangle of branches and leaves overhead.

"Off that sign back there. Giacomo. That's Jack, more

19

or less, in Italian. I like it down there, down by the water. Especially at night. Have you ever heard of people like that?"

"Sure, Jack. Many."

"Most Kendrys don't figure so."

"But *you* do," said Hecker. "Can you tell me, by the way, who's going to contact me at this family gathering?"

"Not that either. It will happen, don't fret." They walked two blocks higher, and then the cat yowled, its hair stood up, and its tail went thick and erect. "Getting close."

The cat yowled again, twisted and jumped to Jack's shoulders and then off into the night. "He doesn't much like Kendrys?" remarked Hecker.

"They're good people, but not much given to gentleness." The thin boy pointed at a rusted and twisted hurricane fence across the street. They were at the rear of a defunct public-school complex, and the school gymnasium was bright with light and noise. "Gate's fallen in. Go on through and down to the gym. Tell your story. Luck to you. I'm no partygoer."

"Okay. Thanks, Jack."

"You have a name?"

"James Xavier Hecker."

"Xavier part is good. I might assimilate that sometime. Goodby." He drifted back and away into the dark beneath the trees, and Hecker headed for the loud, shining gymnasium.

A big woman in a sleeveless leather dress handed Hecker a second piece of fried chicken. "Look at the way she carries herself," she shouted. "Smug, provocative."

"A constant worry to her father," shouted the graying

woman on Hecker's left. "Guerrilla warfare is hard enough without trying to keep tabs on a snooty daughter with a mind of her own." She grabbed an avocado off the abundant banquet table, split it with a knife sheathed on her dappled thigh. She popped out the big egglike seed and passed half the avocado to Hecker. "Eat this, Cousin Jim. You're mighty underweight."

"Just look at her," shouted the big woman. "Straight as a rail and no flesh to speak of. Are they partial to skinny women in your neck of the Republic, Cousin Jimmy?"

Before Hecker could reply, one of the Kendry boys grabbed him away from the food corner of the ramshackle gymnasium and pulled him through half of the several hundred people jammed together on the yellow flooring. "Game, Cousin Jim," he shouted. A six-foot-tall man, a shade over thirty, in a cut-down noga suit, his hair long in ringlets. "We're going to play pumpkin ball."

"Okay by me," Hecker said.

"Bet your ass," shouted the Kendry boy. "I'm Rollo."

"Good to know you, Cousin Rollo."

"Second Cousin," said Rollo. "Eat up that avocado and hunk of chicken and we'll get going. See the basket up there?"

Hecker tilted his head back. Up high in the smoke and haze the old gymnasium basketball goal still hung. "That I do, Second Cousin Rollo."

"The object of this game is to kick the pumpkins up through there. Fun for all concerned." He whacked Hecker and sent him into a circle of eight Kendry boys. Three fat orange pumpkins were huddled in the circle center. "Cousin Jim gets first kick."

"I already have been promised it," said Milo Kendry, who'd introduced himself earlier.

"Bullshit," said Rollo. "Cousin James is our guest, you lout."

"Don't bullshit me," replied Milo. He grabbed up the biggest pumpkin and smashed it on Rollo's head.

"Don't go spoiling the game," said another Kendry. He backed and kicked one of the remaining pumpkins. It rose up toward the metal-raftered ceiling, spun awkwardly, fell toward the musicians' stand.

A dozen Kendrys were on the narrow makeshift platform, playing amplified fiddles and banjos. The Kendry with the hand microphone had been singing a song whose lyrics consisted of the word "stomp" reiterated. The pumpkin dropped on the end of the mike and was impaled there. The singer went on singing.

Rollo snatched a coil of rusty barbed wire out of his jacket pocket, wrapped it around his fist and swung on Milo. He roared, shook pumpkin seeds from his locks, and slashed again.

"You like to give me tetanus, you dummy," shouted Milo. "Lockjaw or something, you dumb bunny." He kicked Rollo in the stomach.

Another Kendry pulled Hecker away from the thwarted game. "Hello, Cousin Jim. I'm your Uncle Fred. What do you think about Jess's last will and testament?"

"You mean Jane's father?"

"Jess left all his possessions to her, he says. I don't think he's been quite right since Jane's mother passed on. Army got her with a new gas they introduced that year," said Uncle Fred. He was broad and tall, but gone to fat. "Insurgents shouldn't have a girl up front. Women are for homebody stuff. You feel like punching somebody around. A woman is handy for that, too. I use to like to stump them, but I'm aging beyond that. Women are okay

22

for stumping but not to lead a band of guerrillas. You getting enough to eat?"

"Yes, fine," said Hecker.

"See these teeth," said Uncle Fred, grinning. "My third set this month. Stole them in a raid on the Santa Monica Sector. These younger kids, their idea of fun is to kick an old man in the face. I don't mind their funning some, but it costs me a set of teeth every damn time. You get old and you get sentimental about your teeth. That will of Jess's, though, is a bad thing. Isn't that the way you see it?"

"I figure Jess knows what he's doing." Hecker ducked a flying fragment of pumpkin.

"This conclave isn't like the ones we used to have," shouted Uncle Fred.

A man with feathery white hair stepped up and tapped Uncle Fred on the bicep. He was a straight-standing man, tall and leathery. "Complaining about something?"

"Just the food, Jess. Food's not like it used to be. Chicken isn't like it used to be. Potatoes aren't like they used to be. Even the lettuce is different."

"You aren't like you used to be either," said Jess Kendry, the leader of the clan and of the guerrillas. He smiled at Hecker. "You're supposed to be Cousin Jim?"

"Right."

"Good to see you," said Jess, holding out his hand. "Be sure you get to say hello to Jane." He narrowed his left eye, said to Uncle Fred, "Jane's a bright girl, a born leader. Fred'll tell you that."

"I already have, Jess."

A grinning Kendry jumped on Jess's back, and Jess, without looking around, bent and airplane-spun the grinning Kendry off and into the nearest wall. "There's my daughter Jane over there. Trot over and pay your respects, Cousin Jim."

Hecker had noticed the girl before, had her pointed out by relatives in the crowd. She was tall, nearly five feet eight, slender. Her hair was darker now than in the days of the Rehab pictures. It was long and straight. She was wearing a pair of boy's tapered khaki trousers and a sleeveless white pullover. Her tan face was slightly flushed. Hecker edged toward her. On the way, someone put a chicken wing in his hand, and someone else punched him in the kidneys. "Thought I'd introduce myself, Cousin Jane," said Hecker.

She had been standing silent, not looking at anything. She blinked her gray eyes, and a slight smile touched her lips. "You're Jim. I had something to discuss with you."

"Oh?"

"Problem of a lost cat."

"His name is?"

"Burrwick," she said. "He spends much of his time down at the waterfront."

"Around Giacomo's?"

"That's him." Her hand touched his arm. "Walk with me over near that exit, and I can talk to you."

"Fine," said Hecker.

She studied his face as they moved toward the arched doorway. "You didn't get hurt here, did you?"

"No, earlier." Hecker had forgotten the traces of the hopper crash on his face.

Jane stopped, back to the wall. "You know," she said quietly, "something about what we're up to."

"You want to topple the Junta."

"And you work for them."

24

"The Social Wing isn't always obliged to agree with the Junta."

"Perhaps," said the girl. "I took a chance on that. The Kendrys and those who've joined us are getting blamed for these riots. That kind of rebellion, burning and looting, I'm not opposed to. If the motives behind it could be used by us. From what I've picked up, these riots won't do us any good. They really are prompted by someone on the outside. Someone who wants to use them against the Junta."

"You sure?"

"I've gathered enough fragments of information to put together a picture," said Jane. "There are people in the Republic of Southern California who think the Junta is much too mild. I'm afraid they're the ones behind the riots in the suburbs. Should they take over, which is a possibility, conditions will grow even worse. Our attempts to get a good government for the Republic will be set back. It's difficult enough now."

"Who," asked Hecker, "do you think is behind these riots and how do they do it?"

"The 'how' I don't know," Jane said. "As to 'who,' the only name I have is not really a name. I keep hearing about somebody called Gadget Man."

"Gadget Man?"

The girl said, "I know where you can start looking for a more definite lead. There's some link between this Gadget Man and Nathan E. Westlake, though I haven't been able to investigate that yet. I feel it's time to bring in someone official on this."

"Nathan E. Westlake, the former Vice-president of the United States?"

"That Westlake, yes. Get to him and investigate. You should find out something."

"He's running that dance pavilion up in the Santa Monica Sector now . . . ," began Hecker. He stopped, frowned at the bandstand.

Jane's glance followed his. "What is it?"

"There, by the music," he said carefully. "That's Second Lieutenant Same."

The girl caught his knobby hand. "The Manipulation Council man. You didn't tell him to come here?"

"No," said Hecker. "I haven't called in a report since I left Social Wing headquarters. They already knew, of course, that I had a contact to make someplace in San Emanuel. There must be a leak in SW somewhere, Same must have had spotters around town waiting for me to show up. Then I was followed here." He looked straight at her. "I didn't set you up, Jane. It is you Same wants, though."

The girl watched his face again. "Yes, okay, you aren't lying. He must have men surrounding us."

"Maybe," said Hecker. "Same usually likes to work alone or with a small complement of men. Tactics he prefers to numbers."

Jane turned, her cheeks hollowing and her eyes narrowing. She caught her father's attention in the crowd and gave him a series of unobtrusive hand signals. "We worked this sign language out when I was a kid. Okay, come this way. There's an emergency exit through that locker room. I doubt he'll try to round up the whole clan. Dad and the boys can fight out of here should they have to." She walked casually toward an archway marked BOYS' LOCKER ROOMS.

Hecker came with her, and in five minutes they were

outside in the night. On a wooded hillside. Suddenly below them a Police Corps hopper, bright-lit and lemon-yellow, came dropping down out of the dark above the gym. Hand torches popped on in the weedy playing fields surrounding the gym. Two dozen at least, illuminating orange tunic sleeves and lime-green trouser legs.

"A raid," said Jane. She hesitated, then pulled Hecker away with her. "Dad can handle this. We'll go wait in our camp."

From behind a white pine a few yards in front of them, a glow of light appeared, flickering on an aluminum pistol. "No one to leave this area now," spoke a Police Corps man.

"It's okay," said Hecker, stepping in the direction of the bobbing hand light. "I'm with the . . ." The blaster crackled before he finished, and his trouser leg caught fire.

Another blaster sizzled from behind him. The PC man's hand flamed in the dark, went black. The aluminum pistol pinwheeled and was lost in the brush. Jane was next to the man as he tottered toward falling. She struck him twice at the base of the skull, and he fell fast and was still.

"How are you?" asked Jane. She looked not at Hecker but at the woods, listening. "No more PC men around here, it seems."

Hecker had slapped the flames out and found beneath the fresh-burnt hole in his pants that his leg was barely scorched. "Nothing. I'm fine. You?"

"Yes."

"He didn't give me time to identify myself."

"Often happens. Come on."

"Where?"

"I told you. To our camp. You can hide out with us for a little."

"I don't have to hide out."

"No, but I suggest we get the hell away from here. Now and fast."

Hecker reflected a second. Then agreed.

CHAPTER 4

Out in center field Hecker paced in a small half-circle, sideways, his big knurly hands on his knees. The sun was straight above, and the rolling field glared green. Hecker watched the big Kendry up at bat and also scanned the area for some sight of Jane. The girl had slipped out of this temporary camp sometime after breakfast. While searching for her, wanting more information on Gadget Man, Hecker had been recruited by Milo and Rollo Kendry to play softball.

The batter hit. The ball came spinning out toward Hecker, but continued on over his head. Hecker trotted after the ball. Beyond this overgrown picnic ground was a wide path and then a synthetic moat. On the other side of the moat rose a stucco mountain, two stories high. A nearly obliterated wooden sign was hanging tentatively to the wrought-iron fence guarding the moat: WELLES PARK ZOO/MONKEY ISLAND. The softball smacked the sign, dislodging it, and then bounced over the moat and came to rest on the island.

Hecker pulled up short of the low rusty ironwork. He knuckled at his shaggy mustache, squinted one eye at the ball. A naked fat girl came out of one of the monkey caves and waved at him with wiggling fingers. "Woowee," she inquired, "isn't it too hot for baseball, cousin?"

"Not for the real aficionado," replied Hecker. "Can you toss me the ball?"

"I'm clumsy in athletics," said the plump girl. She jabbed a thumb in the direction of the game. "Indoor sports for me, if you get my drift." She bent, jiggling, and grabbed up the softball. "We, me and some of my distant boy relatives, are in here having a gang-bang. Keeps you out of the sun on these woowee kind of sultry days."

She was about to toss the ball when a large Kendry boy, clad in the lower half of a suit of thermal underwear, popped out of the murky cave. He whacked the naked girl on her freckled buttocks, and she and the ball rolled down the side of the monkey island and into the moat. Muddy water and dry leaves splashed high. "Woowee," said the Kendry boy, his shoulder-length hair waving. "Now that's humor." He grinned across at Hecker. "There are a lot of humorless bastards in the Republic, cousin."

Hecker said, "No wonder you're hot. That's winter underwear."

The giant boy inserted a thumb under the waistband of the buff-colored underwear. "No, it's a fetish. I can't do nothing without I wear these."

A chubby middle-aged man, bald and blackbearded, came from the cave bent low. "You dumb, creepy bastard," he said. "You go and start playing jokes before I even took my second turn."

"Woowee," said the underwear-clad Kendry. He clutched the complaining man by the beard and pinwheeled him into the murky water. "Oh, that's funnier than the first."

Hecker nodded at the scummy moat water where the bearded man was dog-paddling. "She hasn't come up yet."

"Alice likes to swim underwater. See, this here moat connects with the alligator house over there. Whenever we camp here, Alice does this. Swims underwater over into there and surfaces on the alligator promenade."

"You've thrown her in the moat before?"

"A good joke bears repeating, cousin." He shook his head. "I'm afraid, though, you're not going to find that baseball."

Hecker agreed and jogged back to the field of play. The game had not resumed. Instead, Milo and Rollo were on the pitcher's mound together, battling with baseball bats.

"Tell me I don't know a spit ball, you poor ninny," Milo was growling when Hecker came into hearing range. "I'll smash your unsportsmanlike coco in."

"I'm no ninny, you fat-ass rube," said Rollo, his ringlets tossing. Their bats met with a tremendous clack, and both men quivered. "I've read up on all the major sports. Read in books, you ill-read horsebutt."

Hecker walked on by and across the field and off. There were nearly a hundred guerrillas camped here in this abandoned and unsecured public zoo. Hecker crossed a weathered-wood bridge, searching again for

Jane. As he was passing a partially collapsed merry-go-round, a long, lean man hailed him: "Hey, Hecker."

Hecker joined the man in the fragments of shade that fell from the merry-go-round's glass-and-iron roof. He'd been introduced to him at breakfast. "Hello. You're Hash Sontag. No relation to the Kendrys."

"Right," said Hash. He put two fingers in the breast pocket of his chambray tunic and drew out a little plyo sack. "You're looking for Jane."

"Yes. Seen her?"

"She's worried about Jack, the kid. He was supposed to join us here." Hash shook some flakes out of the sack and into a cigarette paper he'd fished from the back pocket of his tan trousers. "She cut back to see if she could find him. Might be he got picked up in that raid last night. About six others missing, but we don't have word yet on whether they're captured."

"By herself, she went?"

Hash's slate-gray eyes flicked up from their concentration on rolling his cigarette. "Jane needs to be by herself sometimes." Licking the cigarette to seal it, he said, "This is some of that synthetic marijuana they're turning out in the Canal Zone kibbutz. Sort of mild. I know who you are, so you can relax."

Hecker took a back step. "Oh?"

"As was mentioned, I'm not a Kendry," said Hash. He had his back against a poled wooden horse. "Less of them and more people like yourself is what we need. Otherwise, it's always going to be horseplay and the Junta. Not a new government."

"I'm not a recruit."

Hash lit his cigarette and inhaled. He grinned. "You're Sergeant James Xavier Hecker with the Social Wing of the Police Corps. But you're still more on our side than you are on the Junta's."

Hecker said, "Don't expect too much. I'm on an assignment, and it means cooperating. At the end of it I'll go back." He gestured with one rough hand at the tree-thick hills surrounding this small valley. "I'm part of out there."

"At the moment," said Hash. "When Jane suggested getting help from somebody in the Social Wing, I agreed with her. This Gadget Man business will probably need the Police Corps to stop it. We don't have the equipment and facilities. So I figure it's okay to let you help us investigate."

Hecker rubbed at one of the healing cuts on his face. "What do you know about Gadget Man?"

"Only what Jane does." Hash's gray eyes flicked up again. "She's coming down through the trees now. Alone, not with Jack." He inhaled, grinned, drifted away around the far side of the broken-down merry-go-round.

A grass-stained baseball came plummeting from above, accompanied by shards and flakes of dusty glass. Hecker hopped through the wild columbine, yarrow, and monkshood and caught the ball. "The game's resumed," he said.

Jane Kendry was yards away, near one blurred glass-panel wall of the overgrown park greenhouse. "Don't be so patronizing," she said.

Opening the brass grillwork and stained-glass door of the greenhouse, Hecker threw the ball out toward the picnic-ground playing field. "Here you go, Milo."

Jane was wearing tan shorts, a pale-blue pullover, and tan moccasins. She kept dragging one slightly hooked

33

finger down through her auburn hair, giving an angry twist at the end. "Second Lieutenant Same may have Jack."

Hecker made his way over a plank parkway, through wild primroses, zinnias, and milkweed. "I could check in with Social Wing headquarters. See if they know anything. But I'm fairly sure Same must have some way of tapping SW's communications. Since I can refrain from reporting in while I'm on field assignments, I think I will. It's safer at the moment." He got ten feet closer to Jane, and she moved ten feet further away.

"Jack probably got away and went someplace by himself," said Jane. "He's a loner. He's like me. Freer, since he's still really a boy." She hugged herself, her breasts moving closer together. Her shoulders hunched slightly. "I think I may go with you. To check out Westlake. I haven't quite decided."

Hecker said, "Okay. When?"

Jane picked a yellow daisy. "We'll be organizing a raid, planning it today. The actual sortie should be tomorrow. I'm waiting for my scout party to get here. After the raid, two days from now, I'll be able to go to the Santa Monica area."

"I can go now and investigate the former Vice-president myself," said Hecker. "I don't have to wait two days. Just tell me whatever else you know about Gadget Man, about the riots, and I'll move on."

"Why can't you relax, Hecker. Wait." She smiled a slightly puckered smile. "You can't simply go away from here anyhow. You're supposed to be Cousin Jim, remember. Here to help out. There are men posted all around here, watching in all directions. Incoming and outgoing. You couldn't get far."

"The same guys who kept Same away from the conclave last night?"

"No, my own choice," said Jane. "They haven't been celebrating."

Hecker didn't reply.

Jane continued, "You come along on the raid, in my group. If I decide to go along, we can take off from there. If not, it'll be easier for you to get off unnoticed."

Hecker watched the petals from the daisy as Jane tore them free one by one. "Okay," he said. "Your way, then."

"Makes you feel better, doesn't it?" said the pretty girl. "Taking orders. They trained you for that. A yes-sir person they made you into."

Now an arm's reach from her, Hecker said, "Worry about your adopted brother, that's okay. But don't mix me up with what you're mad at."

"Rehab Center crap," said Jane. "Find a reason for this girl's hostility. All the anger. Not the real reason, but some kind of polite sweep-it-under-the-rug reason. Trauma over maternal loss during early pubescent years." She breathed in hard through her nostrils. "They killed her in the street, Hecker. Yeah, it made me angry. Yes, sir. I was quite impressed at the time."

Hecker put a knotty hand on her bare shoulder. "Easy now."

The colored-glass door smashed open and Jess Kendry came in, stepping over bright fragments of yellow, gold, red, scarlet, orange, purple glass. "What sort of tête-à-tête is this, for Christ sake?" he said. His fine white hair was high and tangled, giving his head a bashed-in look. His tan, leathery face was overlaid with a pink flush. "Some kind of incest among blood kin do I see before me? Janey, Janey, what is all this?"

35

Jane reached up and touched the hand Hecker still had on her shoulder. "He'll be okay in a while," she said quietly to Hecker. "Sometimes this happens. Stay back here for a bit." She walked to her father, hunched a little and hugging herself again. "Cousin Jim is only a relative by marriage in the first place, Dad. And secondly, we're just talking about the raid."

"What raid? What raid, Janey?" He tripped among the wild marigolds, stumbled to his knees. "Why do you favor this damn hothouse? It's too hot. It's hot, Janey, this hothouse. Christ."

Jane helped him to rise. "Who have you been with?"

"Uncle Fred and I were up in the elephant house with a couple of bottles of smuggled rye, Janey," said Jess Kendry. "Listen, Janey, this business last night. I'm all spun around. I'm losing my nerve, honey. You see? Listen, Janey, I promised you I'd not let it upset me. Not lose my nerve. Jesus, I can't hold on."

Jane stood straight and put her arm around her father. "Everybody gets frightened. There are real dangers. You know that, and you handled things well last night. It's okay you're afraid sometimes."

Jess began to cry. "No, it's more than that, Janey. I'm so goddam old, Janey. They can kill me so easy now, honey."

"No, they can't," said the girl. She walked him toward the smashed doorway. "You go over to the bunk area and lie down, Dad. I'll wake you for lunch."

"That's a good idea, Janey," said Jess. "I will. Sleep it off."

Piano music sounded out on the picnic ground. A moment later, Milo Kendry appeared in the greenhouse doorway. "Hey, Jess, come on out and play something for us."

"You got a piano out there?" asked Jess, laughing now.

"The twins just dragged it in," explained Milo. "They stole it from a teen-age bordello down in Baja. Smuggled the damn thing all the way up here."

"Those crazy goddam twins," grinned Jess. "Janey, come on and I'll play you a song. I haven't touched a piano in months. That's very thoughtful of the twins. Isn't it, Janey?"

"Yes, Dad. You go on. I'll be there soon." After Jess and Milo had gone, she came back to Hecker. "I'll be with my father for a while. We can talk again later." She left.

Hecker stayed inside the greenhouse even after the music started outside.

CHAPTER 5

The lion house had been turned into a briefing room. A blackboard borrowed from a defunct junior high school was wired up to the bars of one of the shadowy, empty wall cages. Using a carpenter's ruler, Jess Kendry was chalking in a street map. He kept his tongue in the corner of his mouth as he drew the lines, his shoulders slightly bent. On a large square he lettered in MOTHER OF CHRIST HOSPITAL. He paused, rubbed the tip of the chalk against his chin. Then he turned and walked slowly and carefully to the scatter of folding chairs and wooden crates in the center of the vaulted room. Jane was sitting on a tipped slat crate, her knees under her chin, her arms hugging her legs. "I really am sorry, Jane," Jess said. "You know how I get sometimes. Don't be mad."

Jane looked up, but not quite at him. "I'm not."

Hash, slouched in a folding chair labeled DUMLER & GIROUX FUNERAL SERVICES, said, "I heard Milo and

39

some of his buddies talking as if they plan to raise a little extra hell on this raid, Jess."

Jess moved away from his daughter, glanced around at the two-dozen guerrillas in the room. "No more than usual, Hash. We don't have to debate the point any more. We're agreed on the use of a certain amount of terror."

Hecker's wooden chair grated on the decorative tiles of the floor as he put it a few feet nearer to Jane. "I'm just a guest, Cousin Jess," he said. "Still, I had the idea we're raiding this town of San Cabrito for the purpose of getting medical supplies from that Mother of Christ Hospital."

Back at the blackboard, Jess tapped the hospital on the map when Hecker mentioned it. "Exactly, Cousin Jim. However, we like to unsettle the populace if we can. When people hurt, they're more likely to listen. When they listen, then they'll hear what Jane and Hash and some of the rest of us are trying to say. That the Junta is no good. That the Junta has to be replaced by a more democratic government."

Hash began rolling himself a fresh marijuana cigarette. "I think Milo and Rollo and their bunch ought to concentrate on doing their assigned jobs and forget about providing terror for the teen-age girls of San Cabrito."

"There won't be any more incidents like that," Jess assured him. "We've kicked that around enough, Hash. Stop envying the boys their high spirits."

"We need supplies," said Hash, licking the cigarette, "not recreation for Milo and Rollo and the boys. I figure we'd have a smoother raid if we left all the high-spirited fellows here to play softball."

Jess resumed chalking in the names of key streets and buildings of San Cabrito. "We need fifty or sixty men to bring this sortie off right, Hash. The twenty-five of us who do the planning and lead the raids, we need the others. An army can't be . . ."

"All generals. You need privates, too. Foot soldiers and fighting men. Men who think less and fight more," finished Jane. "We know, Father. Just because we have a guest, there's no need to repeat our entire last dozen meetings for him. I'm sure he's seen enough squabbles."

"Right, Janey," said her father. He grinned over at Hecker. "Okay. Here on the run-down stretch of the old Highway 101 is the Police Corps hut. Two and a quarter miles south of the San Cabrito turnoff. There are six PC men there now, according to our scouts. Henry, you and your group have to take them out. The way is up to you. We want no contact between them and the bigger PC stations, and we want no warnings to get out to the Republic of Southern California Army. Keep their PC hoppers on the ground, too. How many is it they have?"

"Three," said Jane. She frowned at the wide, bald Henry Kendry. "I think we ought to talk, very carefully, about Henry's part in the raid."

"He won't repeat last time," put in her father.

"Jane," said Henry, smiling. "Sometimes you're still just a pretty little teen-ager, like you were when they locked you up in the Rehab Center. You get too squeamish, Janey. You cut out all your criticizing now. You and Hash and your new buddy, Cousin Jim."

"You didn't have to kill those three Police Corps men in Redondo," Jane told Henry. "Not *that* way."

"One way, another way," said Henry. He shot up, angry, from his upright orange crate, jabbed a fist in the air toward Jess. "I'm tired of all this bullshit. What's 'guerrillas' mean? Another word for fairies and faggots?

41

We ought to rip up that town, and to hell with a bunch of bandages and aspirins for a bunch of fairies who play sick so they don't have to work."

Hash inhaled on his cigarette. "You're out, Henry. Leave now."

Henry snatched up his crate and came for Hash, swinging it with both big hands. "I don't get bossed around by some hophead pansy."

Pivoting slightly as he rose, Hash avoided the thrust of the wood crate. He jabbed a stiff hand into Henry's neck, and the heavy man slackened, fell to his knees, clutched his crate to him like an accordion, hit the tile with a loud splintering. "We're going into San Cabrito for medical supplies, that's all," said Hash. "Jess, you'll be responsible for delaying the Police Corps boys and taking out their hoppers. I'll be in charge of getting what we want out of the hospital. Jane, you and Jim will head up the group that comes in on the backside of the town and sets up roadblocks to cut off ground pursuit after my group gets the stuff and makes for 101 again."

Jess placed his chalk and ruler on the edge of the lion cage, amidst some dry, dusty straw. "Who voted you in to command, Hash?"

"Father," said Jane, still hugging her knees to her. "We need medical supplies. In this camp and in the others. That's all the raid on San Cabrito is going to be about. No slaughter, no rape. No bullshit."

"Don't talk that way," said Jess. He started toward her. "What's happening, Janey? Nobody cooperates around here any more."

"Cross-purposes," said Hash. He was between Jess and Jane, dragging the unconscious Henry over the smooth floral patterns of the floor.

Jess's leathery face seemed to grow thinner, more wrinkled. "You're right, Jane. We'll do this your way. Hash, when you're through with Henry, you come and outline the raid for us, explain the workings." He walked away, left the room by a side exit.

Jane said, "There's just no way."

Hecker leaned toward her. "What?"

"Nothing," she said.

CHAPTER 6

In the bright, late-afternoon garden, rounded by yellow adobe walls, the brown-robed priest was signing autographs. A dozen people, casual and in their early thirties, stood close by the plump priest, and a score more wandered in the flagstone courtyards and formal gardens of the Shrine of San Cabrito. Immediately at the rear of the smiling priest rose a marble fountain topped by a figure of San Cabrito, who was helping a leper get his footing. Colored water sprayed from the top of the saint's staff, making rainbow patterns in the declining day.

In a patch of shade beneath a transplanted cypress tree, Jane, wearing a blonde wig, sat on a stone bench. On her lap rested a book: *Gourmet Cooking for the Poor* by Father Frederico Caparizzi. Hecker, his back to the autographing Father Caparizzi, stood with one foot resting on the bench. "He cooperates with you?"

Jane nodded, said, "This is another thing you can leave out of your report."

"I'm not obliged to make a formal report to the Social Wing," Hecker told her. "All they're interested in is the riots, and the possible causes of them."

"You can continue on to Santa Monica once night falls and the raid commences."

"You're not going along?"

"No. I decided it's better to stay with my father for now," answered Jane. "Our job here is to set up roadblocks out on Vista Del Mar Road there. With a little help from Father Caparizzi."

"I didn't notice any ocean."

"They filled it in," said Jane. "To build ranch-style homes. Before that, this part of San Cabrito was right on the sea."

"We voted for an artificial ocean," said the blond man who'd been passing, a lean, pretty brunette on his arm. "We're Paula and Jerry Dingman."

"You go around voting in favor of oceans?" Jane stood and moved to the far side of Hecker.

"We lived here in San Cabrito three years," said Paula Dingman, "before we moved to Pedro Loma."

"Every year we'd have a local election, and I would give our okay to having a small artificial ocean built across the street there. I don't actually swim myself, but for the kids."

"The ocean always got defeated," said Paula, smiling.

"Anti-ocean forces are pretty strong here in San Cabrito," said Jerry.

"Lots of the older residents remember that the Chinese Commandos came in across the ocean," explained Paula. She began absently stroking the underside of her right

46

breast. "No ocean, no more invasions. That's how they see it."

"Where we pro-ocean people made our big mistake," said Jerry, "was in trying to get the ocean fluoridated. If we'd gone after a plain salt-water ocean, we might have made it. But for the kids, cavities and all, we decided to go first cabin. Fluoride ocean. And we lost three years running."

"That why you moved?" asked Hecker. He noticed there were still three people waiting for the brown-robed priest's autograph.

"That and the threats," said Paula. She rubbed the alternate breast.

"We began to get a lot of crank calls on the videophone," said Jerry. "Threats. People would ring up and call us water-lovers, describe how they were going to kidnap our kids and drown them."

"Don't forget the perverts," added Paula.

"Perverts took to calling and exposing themselves on the phone screen," explained Jerry. "If you're fast you can flash for about five or ten seconds before the phone company notices and blacks out the call."

"That takes nerve, in a way," said Paula. "You can't use your own home phone because it would be traced. Imagine exposing yourself in a public phone booth while wearing a domino mask."

"We haven't heard from one pervert since we moved down to Pedro Loma."

A white dove came fluttering down over the tile-topped adobe walls of the churchyard and rested for a moment on a dry portion of San Cabrito. "There's one of their famous swallows," said a thin man in a blue jumpsuit.

Jerry Dingman caught the man's arm. "You're mixed

47

up and thinking of Capistrano. It's Capistrano the swallows come back to. At San Cabrito it's seagulls."

The thin man asked, "You mean people get sentimental about when the seagulls come back to San Cabrito?"

"They used to," said Paula. "Except the seagulls don't any more, since the ocean is gone."

"He's free now," said Jane, close to Hecker. "I'll go talk to him." She glided over the flagstones, touched by bright sun and then deep shadow. Hecker grinned at the Dingmans, touched his shaggy mustache in a casual salute, and drifted after Jane.

Father Caparizzi signed a copy of his book for a bronze-tanned Norwegian woman and blessed the flyleaf with water from the fountain at his back. "Bless you, Mrs. Rasmussen. May this book fill you with happiness."

"The ink's running," pointed out Mrs. Rasmussen. She dabbed at the fresh inscription with her paisley bodice-scarf.

"It's the Lord's will, perhaps." Father Caparizzi had a large round face, his hair was a reddish brown, worn long and upstanding.

"I want my husband to be able to read it," said Mrs. Rasmussen. "He doesn't believe I'm here. He thinks I'm over at the Vista Del Mar Retirement Compound having an assignation with a retired napalm consultant."

"He should know that you are dedicated to good works."

"Right, Father. If I was going to sleep around, it would be with poor people."

"Bless you." After Mrs. Rasmussen gave the inscription a final blot and strode off, Father Caparizzi said to Jane, "Is it to be today?"

48

"An hour after sundown." Jane opened her copy of the cookbook.

Father Caparizzi was about to write, stopped, gave a slight gasp. "May the Lord forgive me. I almost wrote your real name here, dear Jane. Too much rests on these humble shoulders, I fear. Two Masses each day, my underground activities, and running a *cordon bleu* soup kitchen. Yet the Lord seems to give me the strength." He put his plump fingers on Jane's. "And recipes."

"Who?"

"The Lord," said Father Caparizzi. "I know you don't believe. Yet I assure you the Lord has appeared to me on several occasions and provided me with recipes for my books. That's His *bouillabaisse* on page twenty-three."

Jane smiled. "What about the cars?"

"For the roadblock? Yes, all here in the wine warehouse off there. You will be careful to set up the block a goodly distance from here? Yes, I'm sure you will. As I wrote you in my last code message, dear Jane, there are five vehicles. None can be traced. Each was brought in separately and under cover of night. One is a quite handsome pre-invasion Chevy. Oh, and one, I neglected to mention before, is shaped like a hotdog."

"A hotdog?"

"Belonged to a meatpacker who used it for promotional purposes before he went bankrupt. I couldn't resist it, because of the food angle."

"As long as it blocks off ground pursuit," said Jane.

"What of the Police Corps hoppers?"

"Dad and his group are taking those out of action."

Father Caparizzi widened his eyes and said to Hecker, "You are a new recruit to Jess Kendry's cause."

"Jane Kendry's," said Hecker.

49

The Police Corps hoppers skimmed the silver lamppole tops, bleating harshly and flashing red. In the doorway of the darkened shrine-warehouse, Jane cried out, "All three, Jim. What happened?"

"Easy now," Hecker told her. There were fifteen of them in the warehouse, ready with the cars to block the road after Hash Sontag and his group passed on their retreat from the raided hospital.

The PC hoppers were still about six blocks distant. Directly below the flickering hoppers were two olive-colored sand trucks. The truck in the lead was Hash Sontag's. He was doing seventy-five, ignoring the amplified warnings from the police ships. Three blocks short of the Shrine of San Cabrito, Hash swung his truck hard to the left. The second truck followed, and the pair went bucketing off Vista Del Mar Road and over gravel and turf and onto a thin strip of synthetic beach.

"He's leading them away from us," said Jane. She tapped Hecker's arm, signaled to the rest of the guerrillas in the warehouse. "Cut the engines, get those cars back under the tarps and straw. Then scatter on foot. Make for the hills beyond here, the woods."

As the figures in the wine-smelling warehouse quickly went about following Jane's orders, Hecker said to her, "Wait and I'll go try to talk to the Police Corps men. Maybe I can do something to help Hash if they catch him. While they're interrogating him."

"They won't question him." Jane scanned the interior of the warehouse, then walked quietly from the doorway, along the dark street by the adobe walls.

"Sure they will if he doesn't get away." Hecker caught up with her, checked back over his shoulder.

An explosion slammed the night, and then flames

bounced up, down on the synthetic sand where Hash had gone. Three more explosions came. Finally a new gusher of fire. The PC hoppers ceased their flashing, their amplified warnings, and dropped down into the fading fire, hovering a safe distance from the burning trucks.

"No survivors," said Jane. "Come on. We can use Tower Hill Road and come out above 101 and near the woods."

Hecker didn't move. The adobe wall he rested his palm against was still holding the warmth of the daytime. "They're," he said, "not supposed to do that. What just happened—to Hash, the others. There are ways of stopping people without that."

Jane continued on, not turning back. "You shouldn't have come this far outside."

A glass Mexican hit the flowered tiles three yards in front of Jane and exploded into a brittle confetti. They were nearing the crest of Tower Hill Road and passing a bright complex of restaurants.

"You okay?" Hecker put his knubbly hand on her slim arm.

"Yes." She was looking up at the balcony of the nearest restaurant. A sign in man-size neon letters said MEXI-EATS VILLAGE! There were two glass *vaqueros* still on the balcony, one flashing orange, the other green. Hopping between them was Milo Kendry. He was being chased by Rollo, who swung a beautiful Spanish guitar. "They never got as far as the Police Corps hut," said Jane.

Through the black, grilled windows of the lower floor of the Mexi-Eats café, a rich orange light showed. A piano was being played inside, and while Jane brushed flecks of colored glass from herself a song began to be sung.

51

Oh, God don't never change,
He always will be God [sang Jess Kendry],
God in the middle of the ocean,
God in the middle of the sea,
By the help of the Great Creator,
Truly been a God to me.

"That's fine," said Jane. She took one of Hecker's big bony hands and squeezed it with both of hers. "It's been getting worse, Jim. Once, well, he's different now. Sometimes. I think, after all, I'd like to come along with you for a while. We'll, well, look for Gadget Man together. Would that be okay?"

Hecker said it would. Then, "What about Jess and the others in there? PC may search the whole town tonight."

"They can take care of themselves." Jane started running. Over the top of the hill. Across the dark, ruined highway. She stepped in among the trees, masked by darkness.

CHAPTER 7

The pale Negro girl tilted back slightly in the straight, green wooden chair and took another shot at the robot. The air-rifle pellet pinged against the robot's humanoid head. "Oh, golly," said the android. "I wish you'd stop pestering me, Juanita."

The girl grinned close-mouthed, made her eyes go wide. She was frail and pretty, wearing a tan pullover and pegged tan trousers, a cowboy-style straw hat on her long hair. When she noticed that Hecker and Jane Kendry had stopped on the narrow roadway and were watching her, she stood, blew imaginary smoke from the air-rifle barrel, and set it aside.

"I guess they're merely being playful," said Jane. She nodded at the dark girl and the blond android in the bright early-morning field of grass.

"Didn't realize it was an andy when we came over the

rise," said Hecker. "If it's her andy, I guess she can shoot at it."

"Let's move on," said Jane. "I know some people on a beach about ten miles down from here. They'll loan us some kind of transportation."

The Negro girl was two hundred feet from them, under the single apple tree in the wide field. Next to her stood a faded red barn. She snatched off her cowboy hat and waved it at them. "Hey," she called, "you want to be interviewed?"

Hecker gave a negative shake of his head. He was about to start walking again along the warm morning road when a chubby man ran out of the barn.

"Hey, Jim." The man was big, with two chins and knobs of fat at his wrists. "Wait up."

Jane asked, poised to move on, "Who is he?"

Hecker said, "He's okay. A guy who used to work with me in the Social Wing. With the Welfare Office now."

"I'll be Anne McRae anyhow," Jane told him. "When you introduce me."

Hecker grinned at her. "Your mother's maiden name."

"That's right. You know all my files by heart."

The plump man arrived puffing, stayed on his side of the field's raw wood fence. "Jim, hello." He reached a fat hand over the top rail. "You on official business?"

"Vacation," said Hecker. "We had some land-car trouble."

"What sort?"

"Somebody swiped it. We're hiking to the next big town to rent one," said Hecker. "Bucky Robb-Collins, this is Anne McRae."

"Hi, Anne," said Robb-Collins. "Look, I can provide you with a ride as far as Motel City. I'm giving a lecture there this noon." He pointed a big thumb at the red barn. "Our bus is in there."

"We'd as soon walk," said Jane. "But thanks."

"No, that's unheard of," said Robb-Collins. "Motel City is the nearest town of any size, and a good ten miles from here at least. It would be unconscionable to allow anyone to walk that distance. Come on, Jim, tell her I'm really sensitive to people's feelings."

"He's got a lot of empathy," said Hecker.

"Thinking of you doing all that walking would give me little pains in my chest and right around here," explained Robb-Collins, tracing an arc on his stomach. "That's why I got out of Welfare Audit, Jim. I kept developing a different pain for each type of hardship case I handled. Malnutrition hurt up here in these bones around the eyes. Worm cases gave me a twinge on this side here. Desertion, which was a rough one, hit me way down here. One day I covered eighteen desertion cases down in the New Watts Sector, and I had to go home and throw up. I quit, and I'm in a much better job."

"What is it?"

"Hadn't you heard? I'm the Riot Commission."

"The whole thing?"

"Yes. Well, me and Dr. Wiggs and our andy, Rex. You remember when the Junta, last month, promised to set up a Riot Commission. I'm what they did. We have a big bus full of research equipment, and we drive up and down the countryside, the safe parts, and interview people and gather statistics. It's great. Especially when the weather is good, like today."

"Why is Dr. Wiggs shooting at Rex with the air rifle?" asked Jane.

Under the apple tree the frail Negro girl had put her

cowboy hat back on. The air rifle was at her shoulder once more.

"Darn you," said Rex. "I'm not kidding, Juanita. You just stop that."

Robb-Collins said, "She thinks he's a fag. Brilliant girl, one of the best Motivational Therapists I've ever run into. Met her when I transferred into Violence Backgrounding after I fled Welfare Audit. She's quirky, is the problem. Anybody she suspects of being at all gay she gets feisty about. So far none of this has held back our research."

Another pellet pinged on Rex. "I'm just going to tell Bucky," promised the android. "Then you'll be really sorry."

"Come on over," said Robb-Collins to Hecker and Jane. "We're pulling out any second. Stopped at this way station for a coffee break and a stretch."

"We'll join you in a minute." When the plump man had gone bouncing back toward the old barn, Hecker said, "We can trust him, Jane. We can ride as far as Motel City, and from there find your friends on the beach."

Jane put one slender hand against her throat. "I don't know."

"We've come a good twenty miles since last night. We might as well ride for a while. Not taking Bucky up on his offer would look suspicious. If not to him, to the girl."

"Okay. For your sake. I'm not tired. It takes more than what we've been doing to wear me down. Didn't it say that about me in my file?"

Hecker frowned for an instant. Then he grinned, and his shaggy mustache uptilted. "Our bus is waiting," he said and swung up and over the fence.

56

CHAPTER 8

"Men have no balls any more," said Dr. Juanita Wiggs. "That's what's causing the riots." She leaned back on her elbows, her slim back against the bus's biggest computer.

"Is this what your Riot Commission has decided?" asked Jane, hunkered in a vinyl deck-chair across from the computer.

"Riot Commission isn't going to find out nothing," said the Negro girl. "Got men running it, men financing it. They're all emasculated. Can't even manufacture a robot who ain't queer."

"Nobody'd have you," said Rex-06896, who was driving the Riot Commission bus. "You're such a darned old nag. That's why you hate men."

"As a girl I used to read of rich matrons jiving with their chauffeurs," said Juanita Wiggs. "Some fun that must have been. Now I got me a chauffeur, and he's a fairy appliance."

"Don't you really have anything on the riots?" asked Hecker. He was at one of the porthole-style windows.

"Nothing but a lot of conflicting opinions," said Dr. Wiggs. She took her floppy cowboy hat off with a circular gesture. "Nobody we interviewed so far admits to nothing. 'Something came over me,' they say. 'I had an uncontrollable impulse to destroy.' Or maybe 'A voice commanded me to burn down the Veterans of the Chinese Invasion hall.' Jive like that."

"You don't accept any of it?"

The black girl half closed one eye and grinned a close-mouthed grin at Hecker. "That's a handsome mustache. Makes you almost manly. No, I don't believe in voices and impulses. I believe in people get mad and they do things. You're in the Social Wing and get around some. Aren't you mad?"

"Not about the same things as the people in the good parts of the Republic of Southern California."

"Juanita," warned Rex over his shoulder, "you better stop making cracks about the Junta."

"I never said nothing."

The tan door leading to the rear section of the bus opened, and Bucky Robb-Collins came back into the main room. "I have to change clothes three times a day, Jim. Sorry I took so long. Enjoying the ride so far?"

"Pleasant view." Hecker nodded at the rolling hills, the green fields and distant pines. "A secured area."

"The Army of the Republic of Southern California has it in hand," said Robb-Collins. "You shouldn't harass Jim, Juanita. His folks started doing helpful things here in the Republic years back. Didn't they, Jim?"

Hecker frowned. "You can hear what we say from the back room?"

58

"Mike picks it all up, yes."

"That's Bucky's fat hobby, eavesdropping." Dr. Wiggs let herself drop into an empty vinyl chair. "This whole bus gives him a thrill. He's practically a gadget freak. Why, he loves this riot job. Gets to play with lots of surveillance and interrogation equipment."

"I don't know what kind of therapy you think you're practicing, Juanita. It isn't working with me, I can tell you."

"She's a natural-born nag." Rex punched two steering-panel buttons, and the bus sped off the road and into a vast cyclone-fenced parking lot. "Motel City."

When they were all out on the gray-topped lot, Robb-Collins suggested quietly to Hecker, "Have lunch here, Jim. After I make my lecture I'll ditch my two associates and join you and Jane."

Hecker caught the fat man's arm and guided him a few cars away. "*Jane*, you said?"

"I know who she is, Jim. I've seen her files in the line of my work. It's okay. I know you Social Wing officers can take action on your own, don't have to cooperate completely with the RSCA or the Police Corps." Robb-Collins glanced at Dr. Wiggs, who was beckoning to him impatiently. "I've found out something you ought to know, Jim. Ought to know before you go on any further."

"What?"

"Not now. Juanita is getting jumpy. Look, I've taken the liberty of calling ahead from our bus phone. I've made a reservation for lunch at one of the motel restaurants."

"No, Bucky. We should move on."

"What I have to tell you is serious," insisted Robb-Collins. "There are fifty-seven motels here and fifty-seven restaurants that go with them. The place I'll meet you is

59

built around a mountain-lodge theme and called The Mayerling. I'll hit there about two. You and Jane relax until then. What I have to say will save you both a lot of future trouble, Jim."

"You could have told me in the time you've taken to give directions."

"Two, then." He punched Hecker's shoulder with a lumpy fist and trotted off to join Dr. Wiggs, who was now chasing Rex through a hopper section of the parking lots.

The lama in the green robe said, "Om mani pad-me hom."

"Beg pardon?" said Hecker as he and Jane crossed the metal-fretwork bridge into Motel City.

The lama was resting with his arms folded on the handlebars of a parked bicycle. "It's Oriental talk," he explained. "That's us up there next to Fort Apache. The Monastery. I'm drumming up trade."

Spreading out before Hecker and Jane were rows of motels. Each covered three acres and had its own theme. The Monastery was built to resemble a Tibetan stronghold. Fort Apache was a nineteenth-century cavalry stronghold, fronted with sand and a sprawled Indian.

"We're only here for lunch," Hecker told the lama.

"Reluctantly," added Jane. She stepped ahead and bent to study the lama's bike. "English, isn't it?"

"You remember England?" The lama was old and faded under his yellow make-up. "Before it merged with Europe?"

"I know English bicycles." A pleased smile touched Jane's face. She tilted her head slightly, said, "I used to visit the Wheelan Studios sometimes, where they used to make motion pictures. Long after it had collapsed, this was. I liked to go there and be by myself. They'd left a whole half a warehouse full of bikes, you know, and somehow the place hadn't been looted much. Bikes and land cars of all kinds. I'd ride the bikes, and I had an English one which was my particular favorite." She looked from the bike to the old man in the lama suit and then around at the vista of motels. "The Wheelan Studios, their sets were more convincing than this."

"Yes, I know," said the old lama. "Still, we do a good business here, year 'round. Our place we stress the Tibet idea, mysteries of the East. Not much about the Chinese angle. You'd be surprised to learn that lots of people in the Republic still hold a grudge against the Chinese because of the Commandos. I say, a man is what he is, and just because he invades your country once upon a time, you shouldn't carry hate around in your heart." He grinned at Jane. "That's sort of an Oriental notion. Some of this rubs off on me."

"We're looking for The Mayerling," said Hecker.

"You'll need luggage. The place is run by a religious group from Santa Monica."

"We're only here for lunch, remember?"

"Right you are. Well, Mayerling is in the center of the layout here. Best way to go is up this way and then left at Yucatan. Go through Sherwood Forest and right when you pass King Solomon's Mines. Watch out for those Robin Hood guys, by the way. They're a little bit gay, if you ask me."

While they were walking by the pyramids and dripping jungle foliage of Yucatan, Jane asked, "What did your friend mean about your parents?"

"Bucky is a compulsive dossier-reader."

A guest van stopped in front of the Yucatan Motel, and

61

a bellhop, dressed as an archaeologist, rushed to meet the arriving guests.

"I know," said Jane. "Are they in the Social Wing some way, too?"

"Both dead," said Hecker.

They continued on into a small shade-spotted forest of oaks and synthetic redwoods. "Well, at least the Army didn't kill them."

Hecker said, "Only one of them."

Jane stopped. "How could you have been cleared for the Security Wing, cleared by the Police Corps and the Junta, with something like that on your record?"

"It's not on my record," said Hecker. "Not everything in my file is exactly true. Now, let's quit on this."

Jane lifted one shoulder. "I always ask a lot of questions when I'm uneasy." She smiled at him, the same kind of pleased smile she'd given the old lama with the bicycle. "Okay." She turned and resumed the trail, striding straight.

Hecker followed. They didn't see any of Robin Hood's men, though there was a green leotard hanging on a low branch off to their left as they emerged from Sherwood Forest.

Jane paused in front of the Gothic Motel, noticing the girl in the long white dress screaming on the second-floor balcony of the turreted country house that was the motel building. The girl held a candelabra. On the wide gray front porch the desk clerk was reaching under his cloak for a packet of snuff.

"How far to Mayerling?" called Hecker.

The man blinked and made the sign of the cross. "Shun that place, sir." He ducked back inside the shuttered motel.

"Authentic," said Jane. "I remember finding a box of Gothic novels in an abandoned town we hid in when I was fifteen. The loveliest quiet town out in the valley. All trees and orchards, birds. I sat out in the woods and read forty-three Gothic novels all that fall." She put her hands about eight inches apart, then pointed a finger at the now empty balcony. "All these books were small and had that girl on the cover. I loved them. I wanted to meet a sinister, dark man so badly. For way into the next year."

They commenced walking again. "Plenty around."

"Not romantic," said the girl. "They have to be tall and handsome. I kept meeting fat, puffy ones like your friend Bucky."

"Easy now. Bucky can be trusted."

"Perhaps."

Mark Twain waved his black cigar at them from the porch of the Stormfield Motel. Around the next corner it seemed to be snowing, the snow rising up from the ground and getting as high as the tops of the thick, frosty pines. Set in among gradually rising hillocks were rustic cottages and a larger chalet with MAYERLING in quiet neon script over its wide wooden door. "Let's have an actual lunch," suggested Hecker. "Not discussing Bucky until he shows up. Okay?"

Jane was moving more slowly. Finally, she said, "Okay, agreed."

The wood door of the Mayerling inn snapped open, and a man came out and fell down the stairs. He stopped in a snowdrift. A middle-sized, and middle-aged, man who looked like a very affable but very tired nine-year-old boy. Sitting up, he showed them a small stamped package. "Going to the mailbox with this." He stood, and the gold keys on the chain around his neck clanked and clattered.

"Welcome to The Mayerling. I'm your host, Tuveson." He sprinted to a pine tree at the corner, which held a blue and gold letterbox. On the way back from posting the package, he fell over into the snow again. Back at the foot of the stairs, he said, "You must be James Xavier Hecker and Anne McRae. Right? Certainly. I'm Tuveson. Your host. Also the chef. Also the wine steward. Obviously. Know what I dropped in the mailbox? Probably not. A video tape of myself. I make them here on the premises. You wouldn't have guessed? Hardly likely. This one is going to the Riot Commission. 'Let's get to the bottom of this unholy mess and find the root cause of the problem plaguing the Republic of Southern California. Enough screwing around. Signed, a friend.' I like to keep my anonymity."

"Don't they recognize your face?" Jane asked him.

Tuveson led them up the steps and opened the door of the inn. "I wear disguises. Naturally. A technique I stumbled onto back when I went in for nasty videophone calls. I was a dirty-phone-call freak for a couple years after I got out of college. I feared for a time they'd perfect this voice-print idea, but our society never got over the collapse of the United States sufficiently to follow up on something fancy like that."

They walked a long pine-paneled hall and entered a large circular dining room that gave a view of snow forests and simulated mountaintops. There were four-dozen white-clothed tables in the room. All empty. "We seem to have avoided the rush," said Jane.

"Do you realize how embarrassing this is to me? Possibly not." Tuveson bumped against the nearest table. "Ours is not, I'll have to admit, the most popular of the sixty-two motels here."

"I thought," said Jane, "it was fifty-seven."

"Well, if you're going to start something like that, I'm through." Tuveson fell over. Got up and stalked out by way of the swing doors to the kitchen.

"How about a table by the fireplace?" asked Hecker.

"Want to stay?"

"We have over an hour until Bucky gets here."

From out of the kitchen returned Tuveson, an ice bucket over his left arm. "Have you noticed I'm changeable? Not yet perhaps. You will. Forgive me for losing my temper. I'll be frank. One reason nobody dines here is my changeable temperament. It's an occupational hazard. Our wine cellar is much too good. Look at this, for instance. A rare vintage champagne. Taylor's New York champagne from 1975. A good year. There was still a United States then. You wouldn't remember. You've heard of New York, though? I'll take Manhattan, the Bronx and so on. Sit down, won't you?" Tuveson stumbled once, righted himself, got the ice bucket set up on a three-legged stand next to their table. "This calls for a better class of glassware. Excuse me, won't you? Obviously, you will." He went again into the kitchen.

"Eighteen-ninety," said Jane. Through the large window a vast and intricate wooden house could be seen rising up beyond the trees and false snow. Jane leaned far to the right. "Yes, and they've got a motel called Nineteen Hundred next to it. All the decades from eighteen-ninety to today. Around in a circle."

"That must . . . ," began Hecker. He stopped, feeling an artificial cold coming from across the empty dining room.

Slowly and stiffly, a long, thin man was coming through a now open window. His face was long and regretful, the exact indoor shade as his moderately gray, seamless suit. He held an alloy pistol in his narrow hand. Keeping it trained on Hecker and Jane, he stepped completely over the sill and in. "I'm pleased to have located you once again." His smile was more a faint sound than a physical expression.

"Second Lieutenant Same," said Hecker.

Tuveson returned, with four champagne glasses on a silver tray.

CHAPTER 9

"I would like," insisted Same in his even, slightly taut voice, "you to turn Jane Kendry over to me, Sergeant Hecker."

"No." Hecker got to his feet and placed himself in front of Jane.

"No, sir, you mean. I am your superior officer, Sergeant Hecker."

"Not actually. Since Manipulation Council is autonomous and not part of the Police Corps, Same."

Moving closer, gesturing with his alloy pistol, Second Lieutenant Same said, "MC automatically outranks everyone, Sergeant. Stand aside. I'm taking this girl into custody."

"You have to have some kind of authorization." Hecker saw that Tuveson was nearing their table.

"I am my own authorization. Jane Kendry is now officially a prisoner of the Republic of Southern California Manipulation Council."

"Let me," suggested Hecker, "call in to the Social Wing and report your request."

"Unnecessary," said the sad, thin second lieutenant. "Give up the girl now, Sergeant Hecker. MC will mail you a receipt."

Hecker bent down as Tuveson stumbled by. Using his right shoulder, Hecker boosted the waiter and spun him into the advancing Same. The tray clanged against Second Lieutenant Same's thin jaw. One of the bright champagne glasses cupped Same's ear for an instant, then fell and smashed on the floor. "Retreat," Hecker told Jane.

She was already up, her slender hands lifting the ice bucket. She took three steps ahead, swung the bucket. The New York champagne fell, ice cubes trailed out, and the metal bucket hit the still off-balance Same hard under his chin. As Second Lieutenant Same clunked to his knees, Jane bent his gun arm over her thigh and wrenched his pistol away. She smashed him across the temple with it, and he dropped sideways, then slammed down and out.

"Another celebration that's getting out of hand," said Tuveson. "No wonder customers shun us. Too much violence. Even with such a nice stock of wines."

"For a few minutes," Jane ordered him, "be quiet."

"Why don't you lock me in the wine cellar?"

"Lock yourself. Get going."

Tuveson hurried, stumbling, off.

"Well?" Jane asked Hecker.

"Let's continue," he replied.

"You can get off here." Jane's pretty face was slightly flushed. "Tell Same I used a weapon to make you stick with me."

"We're looking for Gadget Man," said Hecker. "We'll find him. Out the window. Let's go."

Jane ran to the window that showed the circle of decade motels and opened it wide. "Won't the Social Wing disapprove of your leaving an MC man flat on his ass in Motel City?"

"Once I finish my job," Hecker said, "I'll file a report on Same. Despite what you think, SW doesn't let stuff like he's been trying go unquestioned." He waited until she'd jumped out into the false snow, followed.

"Your friend," said Jane, running toward 1900, "Bucky must have called in to Manipulation Council."

Hecker said, "Yes, that occurred to me. Same found us fairly easy."

In a gingerbread garage next to the registration gazebo of the 1900 Motel, a four-and-a-half-foot-tall man was loading plyo sacks of dirty laundry into an antique electric automobile. "They won't let us have a laundry room, no," the man said when he noticed them in the garage. "Say it's an anachronism. Every day I've got to haul all the dirty linen over to Nineteen-sixty to wash. Kee-*rist.*"

"We'd like," said Hecker, "to borrow your car."

"Oh? Kee-*rist,* don't ask for it now. Wait until I take this stuff to the Day-'N'-Nite Laundromat, huh? Otherwise, I'll have to carry it all by hand to Nineteen-twenty, where they've got a washing machine and a clothesline."

Jane made a pie-size circle in the air with the pistol. "We need a car right now. The keys."

The small man dropped the sack of stained sheets and fished a ring of keys from his vest pocket. "Big one in the middle. Why're you swiping this heirloom anyhow?"

"For a getaway." Hecker helped Jane into the passenger seat.

"Oh? That's sort of exciting," said the small man. "That's a break in the routine. Usually it's mostly laundry and anachronisms around here."

Hecker swung into the driver's seat, figured out how to get the ancient land car going. They drove away from 1900, and in five minutes were free of Motel City and on a back highway heading in the direction of Santa Monica.

Hecker shouldered the car a few feet further into the forest of dark pines. "No sign of air surveillance yet, and it's been an hour."

"Maybe," said Jane, her back against a tree bole, "Second Lieutenant Same doesn't want the Police Corps in on the kill."

"He doesn't want to kill you, Jane, or anyone."

"I keep forgetting," the slender girl said. "We're only about twenty miles from Santa Monica, Jim. We can hike on these back roads until sundown, and then borrow transportation for the rest of the way to Westlake's dance pavilion."

They'd walked a half mile on a dirt road when someone called, "Well, what a pleasant surprise. Hi, folks."

Up a hillside some thirty yards was a cleared space in the woods. A shield-shaped sign designated it an RSC Free Roadside Park. Seated at one of the three simulated redwood tables were Jerry and Paula Dingman, the couple who'd been at the Shrine of San Cabrito. "Hello," called Hecker.

"Hiking?" asked Paula. She was wearing white shorts.

"Had some car trouble," Hecker told the smiling couple.

70

"It's recurrent," said Jane.

"We gave up on land cars," said Jerry Dingman, who was in a one-piece tanksuit-style hiking costume. "They're unsafe. Slipshod, too. We never could get one where the stereo worked right. Ours would always play the tapes backwards. We have a family hopper now."

"Only two crashes in four hundred air hours." Paula had a small circle of insect bites next to her left nipple, and she was absently rubbing at the spot.

"Come on up and join us for a glass of proteinade or an ale," invited Jerry.

"Well," said Hecker.

"They're okay," said Jane quietly to him.

"How do you know? After Bucky."

"I get hunches. Like I did with you. Their suburb, remember, is Pedro Loma. About two miles above Santa Monica. We'll get a ride with them."

"Okay," said Hecker and climbed up the hillside. "You folks heading our way? Toward Santa Monica? Looks like our land car will be in the shop for a week, and we're stuck."

"Yes, as a matter of fact," said Jerry Dingman. "This is the last lap on our vacation. We'll give you a lift. Paula and I should be pulling up camp in, oh, roughly, half an hour."

"As far as the outskirts of Santa Monica," said Jane, "would be fine."

"We only have to make one stop first," said Paula.

"That's right," said her blond husband. "At a pot-luck supper in the Rancho Dos Passos suburb. About fifteen miles from here."

"We wouldn't do it, since we're pretty worn out, as

71

you might imagine, except it's for a fund-raising thing."

"For a good cause," said Jerry.

"It's to stop some conservatives from ousting a liberal teaching machine," said Paula.

CHAPTER 10

A half hour before the riot, Hecker was being told about the suburb of Rancho Dos Passos by a retired nerve-gas publicity man. Rancho Dos Passos was grassy hills, low L- and T-shaped houses of tinted glass and white metal. From the red-tile patio of the publicist's home, Hecker could look clear through the house and see the forest of pines sloping away across the road.

"Once I realized," Bryson Whorf was saying, "the root source of my unease, I was able, fortunately, to do something. You see, I realized I was trying to sell a product I didn't really believe in. Making, you see, for tension. I was getting these little pains all in through here."

"There's a lot of that going around." Hecker selected a nearbeef-on-soy sandwich from the buffet table.

"For me, you see, the moment of truth came in a hovercraft. An odd place for an insight, but nevertheless, there it was. Insights are like orgasms. You can't always control

73

them or tell where you're likely to have them. We were up there testing a new nerve gas on some rioting farm labor in the Fresno Sector, and I suddenly said to myself, 'Bry, this is a dirty business. You ought to quit.' I did, soon as we landed." Whorf was a lean, shaggy man, with a large, sharp face. He poked his finger into various parts of himself as he talked. "Now I support liberal causes and help the arts."

Jane returned to Hecker's side, touched him. "How so?" she asked their host.

Whorf poked himself in the navel. "If you have time later, I can show you around our community. We'll have to go by land car, since I never go up in a hopper or any aircraft any more."

"Why is that?" asked Jane.

"Tell us," put in Hecker, "about local art."

"In answer to your question, Miss McRae, I was telling Mr. Hecker here that I haven't always been a liberal and a champion of the underdog," explained Whorf. "Once I was a public-relations man for the nerve-gas industry."

"Oh," said Jane. She wandered away to another part of the moderately crowded patio.

"A lot of people still react that way," said Whorf. "But, you see, the past is over. Once I dropped nerve gas on *braceros* and wrote, produced, and directed prize-winning documentaries for the industry. Now I help our Rancho Dos Passos community finance things like that beautiful all-night tennis court down the road. I've invested heavily, too, in the Cinema Hut, which provides a growing and avid segment of our neighbors with film classics. Southern California, you see, was once the capital of the motion-picture industry. If you two are going to be here tomorrow, you won't want to miss the start

74

of our John Agar Film Festival. A wonderful minor artist from the nineteen-fifties and -sixties. Tonight there's a panel discussion on Porky Pig."

"We'll have to miss both events." Hecker grinned without disturbing his mustache and went toward Jane.

The slim girl had just taken a gibson from a tray and was listening, with three other guests, to the controversial teaching machine.

"Ach," said the machine, which was human in shape but painted an olive-drab shade, "der trouble is dat der school is too conservative yet for zum uff mine notions. Yah?"

"Now, Hans," argued a middle-sized and balding young man, "don't try to rake that up again, because it simply is not so. The Everyman Condominium School here in Rancho Dos Passos is one of the most liberal in the whole Republic of Southern California."

"Zo? Dot ain't saying much maybe."

A plump woman in a silicone-treated paper dress said, "Hans is right, Dr. Purrletsky. You're deluded because you're the principal of Everyman. I think your admissions policy is dreadful, narrow."

"Yah, yah," said the teaching machine.

"For instance," said the plump woman, "when our Fairplay for Commandos Committee petitioned you to allow Chinese Commandos to attend Everyman, you balked, refused, Dr. Purrletsky."

"Anna-Maria," said the Everyman president, "the City Council had a valid objection. Nobody has seen a Chinese Commando for years. They'd be pretty old if one did show up in Rancho Dos Passos."

"You're trying to mix morality with logic again," said Anna-Maria. "I think the reputation of Everyman would

75

have gone up if you'd gone on record as being in favor of a fair deal for Chinese invasion veterans."

Purrletsky shook his head. "I didn't want to annoy the Junta over something so abstract and, as was decided by a 5-to-1 vote, trivial."

"Der Junta," said Hans. "Dose guys ought to be taken out und shot. Yah?"

"It's that kind of talk that got you in trouble, Hans," warned Purrletsky.

"Dot's right. Because I figured out how to program mineself. Yah?"

"What's so fair about your admissions policy anyway?" demanded Anna-Maria.

"Well, for a junior college I think we're quite liberal," said the Everyman head. "We started off in our first year admitting students no matter what their race or creed. Then we voted that high-school grades were not important, and shortly thereafter to even allow kids in to Everyman who hadn't made it through high school. Next we liberalized our admissions further to allow kids who hadn't even gone to high school to enter Everyman. We next ruled, under pressure, that age was not a factor in admissions. We now admit any kid over six who wants to come, and the vice-president of the sophomore class is a ninety-six-year-old Hindu. We now even have eleven toddlers in frosh English, and last semester a one-legged grandmother captained the football team. What's all that if not fair?"

"No Chinese Commandos," said Anna-Maria. "And, furthermore, not one course giving students the Chinese Commando side of the invasion."

"You've got me there," admitted Dr. Purrletsky. "I tried to have the Chinese Commando cause treated more fairly in our Collapse of America course. I'm afraid, though, if I insist too strongly the Junta will step in."

Anna-Maria said, "I hear that at Pomona Everybody's College they teach Chinese Commando philosophy and tactics in Collapse of America 2A."

"They did until Manipulation Council shot the instructor," said Dr. Purrletsky.

"Dot's only a rumor," said Hans the teaching machine. "I tink it vas just vun of der students fooling arount."

"This was a sophomore class, Hans, and kids aren't allowed to go armed to class until their junior year. That's the rule at Pomona."

"Vell, I tell you something. Maybe I stop messing around mit you humans und get mine own people behind me."

"Meaning who?"

"Der machines, who else?" Hans raised a mechanical fist. "Maybe I march on der Junta capital, right in Sam Yorty Square, mit a few hundred servomechanisms und androids. Dose Junta guys vould tink tvice if dey see me strutting down Spring Street mit two hundred angry refrigerators marching behind me. Yah?"

"What about the guerrillas?" asked Jane, setting her empty glass on the edge of a coppered barbecuing unit.

"Vot?"

"Why don't any of you feel concerned about the guerrilla army, about the people who are really doing something?"

"We'd better not go into that topic, miss," said Purrletsky. "Some subjects are, after all, too touchy to chat about right out in the open."

"Oh, bullshit," said Jane.

77

"Easy," said Hecker. He took her hand, but she jerked free.

Anna-Maria suddenly grabbed the barbecuing cart, slammed on its fire buttons with her fists. "She's right. Everybody talks too much in this dumb town." She hefted the heavy machine up and threw it smack into a glass wall. Bryson Whorf was down on his knees clawing up patio tiles. When he clutched up an armful he jumped into his next-door neighbor's yard and started tossing. The other guests, except for the Dingmans, who stood looking upset, began to grow violent. Jane ran into the Whorf house and ripped down draperies.

Hans looked at Hecker. "Mine Gott, it's here. Der riot fever."

Hecker started after Jane. Dr. Purrletsky tackled him just short of the house, punched him in the side. "What a lousy-looking mustache that is. I meant to mention it earlier."

Hecker kneed him gently in the stomach and rolled out from under. "Jane," he called, rising.

All the wood furniture of the living room and dining room was piled on the Arabic rug of the living room and was starting to burn. Jane was not here and Hecker passed on through.

From the flagstone front porch, Hecker thought he saw her running downhill. A truck shaped like a potato jumped the curb and came churning at him. POTATO HEAVEN/101 KINDS OF FRIES, it said on its side. Hecker pivoted, avoided the rush of the truck, and was on the sidewalk when its front end smashed into the glass wall of Whorf's dining room. All the lights in the night tennis courts went suddenly out, and he heard rackets being stomped on and nets ripped. Fires were blossoming all

78

around, yellow and black smoke spiraling up into the night. At a distance, blasters were crackling. A whomping explosion sounded.

Hecker saw a torch flung at the lodge-style Cinema Hut, and he caught a glimpse of Jane. She was racing now and went around the side of the building. Someone was up smashing the marquee, and the foot-high letters A, G, A, and R fell around him on the pavement as he jogged by.

Behind the Cinema Hut the forest began. Hecker tried to listen for sounds of Jane. He thought he heard Jane moving quickly into the woods, but the riot growing in the suburb killed most small sounds. He put one bony fist against his mouth for a second, then decided to track her this way in the forest.

CHAPTER 11

She wasn't here, either. Hecker could sense that as he came, alone, down the tangled path. The trail rambled downhill through a forest of thick oaks. The night cold and the night dark were fading, and Hecker stopped, rested against a massive tree trunk. The bones in his face still seemed to hum with the chill of the misty woods, the joints in his big hands ached. Hecker massaged the bones beneath his ears with his stiff fingers. When he took a deep, chill breath, he felt a jab of dizziness. He had been at this most of the night, searching for Jane Kendry. Tracking, calling her name when he thought it safe to call, listening.

Dawn was coming on, and the forest grew a whitish blue. From below came the sound of metalware rattling. Hecker resumed his descent. The woods thinned out and then ended on the lip of a ridge. Two hundred feet below was a rocky stretch of beach, gritty gray in the morning light. This was another unsecured piece of the Republic. Some forty or more people were down on the beach, most of them still asleep, twisted in old blankets, RSC Army sleeping bags. A six-foot-long Negro girl was sleeping naked on her back at the very edge of the sand, the surf brushing at her relaxed left hand. By a growing cook fire a fat woman in an *art nouveau* tent dress was crouching beside an antique aluminum coffeepot. This band of scavengers had much more stored on their portion of beach. Boxes and crates were piled up between the scatterings of sleeping people. Plyo-wrapped bundles of newspapers and magazines were stacked high along the scrub at the hillside end of the beach. Dune-colored plastic barrels, a good hundred of them, made a snaking row just beyond the furthest reach of the tide.

Something was jabbed hard into Hecker's side. He'd been kneeling on the edge, watching the scavengers. Turning, he saw a small, slightly overweight man in his mid-thirties. The man was bent down with one hand against Hecker's lower ribs. He was bushy, bearded. "You're not a nostalgia freak," he said in a slightly questioning tone.

Hecker twisted and saw the hand that had jabbed the object at him. "You're not even armed. What is that?"

"It's a bisque Mickey Mouse doll," said the hairy man. "I'm just back from the Burbank Territory, and I was able to get my hands on a dozen of these babies. Isn't it lovely? I'm a Disney freak."

"A what?"

The man made a dry sound with his tongue. "No, first explain who you are. Our lookout is dozing, or you wouldn't have gotten even this close."

"Did you see a girl the way you came? Tall, pretty,

wearing a blonde wig. Or she may be auburn-haired again."

The man put the six-inch-long doll carefully into a knapsack on his sweatered back. "Saw nobody. Who is she?"

Hecker, after hesitating, said, "Jane Kendry. There was a riot in Rancho Dos Passos, and we got caught in the edges of it and were separated."

"You," said the small, bearded man, "don't look like the law or the military to me. No, and I'm good at making quick judgments. I have to be to make a go of the nostalgia business. I'd estimate you're not Police Corps." He held out his hand. "My name is Pierce G. Wiersbecky. I don't have time to be active in the guerrilla movement. Hunting down stuff for my nostalgia-freak customers uses up all my time. Still, I'm sympathetic to Jane Kendry. Come on down and have breakfast."

"I should keep moving."

Wiersbecky studied Hecker for a moment more. "You look groggier than I do. Rest a little. I got in a tangle with a roving band of Disney scavengers out in Burbank. It was a real problem, and I had to run. Those guys haunt the area where the Disney Studios used to be, even though the Republic of Southern California keeps it under guard. You never heard of Walt Disney?"

"In school." Hecker stretched up, yawned.

"I've got the biggest selection of Disney freak stuff in the RSC. I heard of one guy, Bill Van Horn, up in the Frisco Enclave, who has more items, but they don't have to hide out from the law up there. Considering my handicaps, I'm the champ."

"You like the stuff yourself?" They started down the hillside toward the sand.

"No, it's all crap to me," said Wiersbecky. "My personal tastes run to some of the lesser-known animators of the nineteen-forties. If I had a choice, I'd retire and become an Andy Panda freak."

"What route did you travel coming back here?"

"Through the woods the last couple of miles. Didn't see any sign of Jane Kendry. The trail I usually use follows the line of the beach. Before that, I was on an unsecured piece of the old 101. Quiet there, though you have to watch out you don't get shanghaied by press gangs from the Baja bordellos."

"They hunt this far now?"

"Sure," said Wiersbecky, walking on sand now. "Lot of those male madams are gadget nuts, and they come into RSC because we have more hardware stores."

"Hardware stores?"

"That's what the gadget freaks call a place where they can get what they want," explained the bearded man. "It's like a whorehouse for the mechanically inclined. Slang."

"Must be new." Hecker hadn't heard the term yet in his Social Wing work. "Ever hear of somebody they call Gadget Man?"

Shaking his head, Wiersbecky motioned Hecker to approach the big woman in the *art nouveau* sack. "No, I don't know. That name means nothing. As I said, I specialize in Disney freaks. It's cleaner. Mama Lemon, this is a friend of Jane Kendry."

The woman was puffy, weighed over two hundred and fifty pounds, and was an eggshell color. "I'm Mama Lemon. I run this nostalgia operation. Who are you?"

"James Xavier Hecker."

"Doing what?"

84

Hecker looked out at the brightening ocean, where seagulls were sitting and loitering in the water. "I'm with the guerrillas."

"Has Jane Kendry been by here, Mama Lemon?" Wiersbecky shrugged out of his pack. "They got lost from each other during a riot."

"Suburb riot?"

"Yes, up in Rancho Dos Passos. Do you know Jane?"

Mama Lemon smiled, touched the perking coffeepot with two puffy fingers. "Sure." She pressed the same two fingers against her lips, her eyes squinting. "Is he to be trusted, Pierce?"

"Look at these lovelies," he said. "Mickey, Minnie, Goofy, Uncle Scrooge, Huey, Dewey, Louie. Boy, if I had been able to snag a Donald Duck, I could get two hundred bucks for Donald and the nephews."

"Him I'm asking about."

"He's okay," said Wiersbecky. "I'm never wrong on appraisals."

Mama Lemon poured three cups of coffee. "Real coffee," she told Hecker. "We got a produce-tycoon customer who's a freak for Bob Dylan LPs. You know, they pressed millions of those in the nineteen-sixties and -seventies. You can't find hardly one in RSC."

Hecker took the cup of hot real coffee. "You were going to tell me something about Jane Kendry."

"Come over here," said Mama Lemon. She led him to one of the olive-drab barrels. "Hold it a sec. Hey, Mozelle. Wake up."

The naked black girl had rolled over into the surf and was slowly slipping underwater. She sat up, blinked. "Huh. What time is it?"

"Breakfast. Don't go drowning." Mama Lemon reached

85

into the barrel and took out a rolled-up poster. It was sheathed in clear plastic. "The sea air ruins this crap if you don't protect it. Look here." She uncased the bright poster, unfurled it.

"So?"

"Wheelan Studios," said Mama Lemon. She pointed to the motion-picture studio's name and emblem at the bottom of the poster. "See, right here, next to the gorilla's foot. They made this *Faster Faster Affair* movie this poster is advertising. Wheelan Studios. They used to be right up the coast here. Not more than five miles from where we're standing right now."

"Wait," said Hecker. "Jane mentioned something about an old movie studio she used to visit. Run-down place, closed up. A place she went to when she wanted to be alone."

"Wheelan Studios." Mama Lemon allowed the poster to roll itself up. "I'm the one who told her about it, took her there the first time. Jane I've known on and off a long time. Also Jess. Maybe you can look at the Wheelan Studios for her."

"I'll try it."

"Sit for a bit first. You're short on sleep."

"Yes."

"Finish your coffee," said Mama Lemon. "Tell Jane, when you see her, I said hello. We'd like to help her more, but this business takes all our time."

"Good Christ!" shouted the black girl.

Coming over the rim of the hillside above were a half-dozen Police Corps men on foot. The scarlet bands on the sleeves of their blue-and-gold uniforms indicated they were with the Beach Patrol. Three of them carried

86

blaster pistols. One held a rifle. The other two had flame guns.

"They've come to hit us and our stock," cried Mama Lemon. "Everybody scatter."

People began running. A few of the scavengers were still not awake. They rolled out of blankets and sleeping bags, puzzled, half asleep. The PC men commenced firing. The crackling blasts were high, meant to frighten. The flame guns opened up next, striking straight at the cartons and barrels. The plastic bags withered to black, and everything began to burn.

"Let us move it," yelled Wiersbecky at the Police Corps men. He went dashing toward them.

Flame splashed off a plastic barrel and tore at the bearded man. He started to burn up—his beard and his clothes.

"Stop it," said Hecker. He headed for the spinning-with-pain Wiersbecky.

Mama Lemon jumped and grabbed Hecker. "Up into the woods," she ordered. "They'll finish him for sure. No chance."

Wiersbecky screamed. The PC men with pistols circled him, firing. The burning man was slammed into the air, fell back into the ocean.

Hecker spun, slipped on the gritty sand, made for the hillside. He clutched at scrub and brush, tearing his skin on thorns and sharp leaves as he climbed. He moved fast and was soon in among the trees. He ran on. He was ten minutes from the beach, alone again, before it occurred to him he hadn't tried to identify himself to the Police Corps. He kept running.

87

CHAPTER 12

An adding machine was clicking in among the cedar and laurel trees. Hecker stepped from the noon glare of the old two-lane road and into the straight up-and-down shade of the forest. A few hundred feet in among the trees, and he saw three slim young girls kneeling around the deep-brown trunk of a cedar. The youngest of the three, a pale-blonde girl of about fourteen, had her legs straight out in front of her and a small battery-powered adding machine on her lap.

"We all already agreed," she was saying, "not to count him."

The freckled brunette shock her head angrily. "The heck we did. I say it counts."

"No, Barbie," said the third, a tall, black girl, "you change the rules just so you can win."

"I don't. You guys do."

"You're being very childish," said the girl with the adding machine. "Maybe you ought to go back to collecting autographs, Barbie."

"I say my score is eight," insisted the brunette.

"Barbie, you don't get a point for simply getting in bed with him," explained the pretty Negro girl. "You got to make it. That's the rules. If we relaxed the rules, then anybody could rack up points. Just jump in bed with a morality player and out, and say, 'Whee, I got another point.'"

Barbie said, "Well, I still don't believe you got twelve points."

"*I* do," said the black girl.

The blonde with the adding machine said, "Stop this bickering, Barbie, or we'll disqualify you. The acting festival is going to be here at the campground another whole day. If you really try, you can maybe at least tie."

"I don't know, Angie. You got ten, and Elverneta has, my gosh, twelve. There isn't much use trying."

"But you have seven," Angie pointed out. "You should be able, by really trying, to make it with five more morality players before noon tomorrow. After all, there are six acting troupes at this festival. Over a hundred guys."

"Yes, but there are twenty fan clubs here, too. Five hundred girls or more."

"Hardly any of them are as attractive as you," said Elverneta. "If you were more positive, Barbie, you could ball anybody."

"I try my best."

Angie tore the paper tape from the adding machine and noticed Hecker, who had come up to within five feet of them. "Hi, are you a morality player?"

"Trouble," said Barbie.

Hecker looked at the girl. "You're Barbie Reisberson,

90

aren't you? I worked with you in the South Pasadena Sector."

The brunette girl, head down, said, "That's right, Sergeant Hecker. School problem. I was wandering off."

"You're wandering further now."

"No. I don't wander now, because I don't go home any more."

"Sergeant? Is he a P-Cop?" asked Elverneta.

"Not exactly Police Corps, Social Wing," Barbie told her. "He's not a bad guy, for somebody his age and situation."

"Why are you here, Barbie?" Hecker asked the girl.

"There's a festival."

"What sort? Acting, did you say?"

"Morality plays," said Angie, sliding the machine off her lap and standing.

"Oh, yeah," said Hecker. "You're talking about the mechanized-morality-play people. Groups like Captain Nazi and his Motorcycle Minstrels. We've been getting complaints about him and his Brute Theater movement."

"He started it, yes," said Barbie. "But, boy, now there are all kinds of guys in it."

"Captain Nazi and his bunch are here, though," said Elverneta, laughing. "They're still the best."

A gray squirrel, startled, ran across Hecker's left foot. "Have you seen a girl, a girl in her twenties, tall and probably blonde, pass this way?" Hecker asked the three girls.

"You don't find many Brute Theater fans over twenty," said Elverneta. She rested one palm on her hip. She was wearing tan shorts and a white noga doublet. "Say, aren't you going to lecture Barbie? You're a social worker, aren't you?"

91

Hecker drew his forefinger across his mustache. "Yes. I've already, though, said everything I had to say to her."

"Trying to put her on her honor now, huh?" asked the dark girl.

"I'm . . . ," began Hecker.

"Happy noontime," shouted the giant man who leaped into their midst. "Happy cedar trees to one and all. Christ, isn't all this lovely?" He snatched Elverneta by her hip-resting hand, yanked her to him. After tossing her three feet up stiff, he caught her by the elbows and kissed her. "Happy sunshine, all." He flat-handed the Negro girl away, laughed, nodded at Hecker. "I'm Isaac Walden, better known as Captain Nazi, actor. Happy pine cones to you. Happy blue sky. Christ, isn't the world beautiful?"

Hecker said, "I'll be moving on."

"He's a P-Cop," said Elverneta. "Social Wing."

"Happy civilian clothes," said Captain Nazi. He had a rich red beard and a bright bald head. A sleeveless noga jacket that had been hand-painted to resemble chain mail. Black cowboy pants and aluminum-plated boots. A gun with the red leather holster hanging in mid belt over his groin. A synthetic ruby in his left nostril and a tiny swastika flag as an eyepatch. "You look like a terrific guy, anyhow. I tell you what . . . Who are you, anyway?"

"Barbie knows," said Angie.

Captain Nazi covered the brunette's left buttock with one big hand, squeezed. "Introduce us. God, but people are all so lonely. I want to know them, each and every one."

"Ouch," said Barbie.

"James Xavier Hecker," said Hecker.

"Welcome, Hecker," said the captain. "Happy laurel

leaves to you, happy goldenrod pollen. Happy flickering squirrel tails. I'm going to give you a freebie. A complimentary ticket to this afternoon's morality play."

"No, thanks. I have to get on."

"The title of this afternoon's uplifting allegory," the wide captain told him, "is *No Jelly Roll for King Arthur.* The purpose of motorcycle moralities is to reform and inform while entertaining. For that purpose I formed the Brute Theater, and I have been touring successfully for nearly a year. Have you read my reviews?"

"No, but I've seen the police reports." Hecker took a step back. Four large arms grappled him.

"God bless," said Captain Nazi. "You've just been auditioned, evaluated, and recruited into the Brute Theater. We need, since we seem to use them up so fast, somebody again to play the part of the Devil."

The two Brute Theater actors who'd snuck up on Hecker lifted him now from the ground and began twining him in ropes and chains. "Is it a speaking part?" asked Hecker.

"No, but if you groan real well you can upstage us."

"You shouldn't," said Barbie softly.

"Shouldn't what?" asked the captain.

"Nothing."

"Happy captivity," said Captain Nazi.

The outdoor clearing seated about six hundred, most of them young girls, bright-eyed, tensed in their kneeling positions in the dirt, fists expectant against breasts. Roaming the audience were young actors from the other companies in the festival. Hecker was tied to a pole at the edge of the low canvas-covered platform that served as the stage.

93

Captain Nazi had donned a heavy, gold crown and had a sword hanging in place of his pistol. Standing at the edge of the canvas, one big hand fisted against his chin, he was in the midst of a soliloquy. "What, then, shouldst I do, O angry gods? I am tore with speculation and know not howst I ought proceed."

A shaggy actor in a cloak entered from the trailer parked just behind the stage. "Hail to thee, blithe King Arthur, destined to be ruler of all this green and pleasant land. I am the Spirit of a Steady Job and wouldst woo thee into the secured towns."

Captain Nazi struck his chest. "O, I am sore tempted."

"Don't sell out, baby," cried a hundred girls.

"I offer thee, noble monarch of the forest," said the hooded figure, "a desk near a window, a three-bedroom house, a tall wife, two sons in the upper ten percent of their class. Thou hast but to sign this contract, good King Arthur."

"Nay, nay," roared Captain Nazi. "O gods of noble purpose, give me strength to resist this tempting offer."

"Stomp him," cried a red-haired girl in the front row.

Captain Nazi extended a spread-fingered hand toward her. "Yet, hark! I seem to hear the gods. They speakst to me of what I must needs do."

"Stomp him," shouted a dozen girls, bending toward the big actor.

"Stomp him," yelled two hundred more.

"Aye! The gods, who determine our fates with a toss of the dice, has spoke." Captain Nazi clomped toward the dark-robed actor, leaped into the air, and hit him full in the stomach with his aluminum boots.

"Aiiee!" roared the Spirit of a Steady Job. "I had not expected an argument of this nature." He snatched at

Captain Nazi, got an armlock on him, and tosed him flat on his back.

"Zounds!" said the captain. "Down but not out, for my heart is pure." Still on his backside, he booted his opponent in the groin.

The cloaked man doubled.

Next to Hecker a girl's voice said, "Here. A knife and, I hope, a key that'll work on the padlock. They're all watching the tussle." Barbie had slipped out from behind the trailer.

"Thanks," said Hecker as the brunette dodged away out of sight again.

The Spirit of a Steady Job was down now, with Captain Nazi jumping on his stomach. "Right and justice will always triumph, a maxim we wouldst do well to bear in mind."

"I've seen mock battles, but this is the mockest," said a blond-haired Negro actor from the audience. "Gay almost."

"Sit down," called some of the girls.

"Wait till the Knights of the Mojo Acting Brigade gets up there, young ladies," said the black actor. "These fairies will look like the pansies they are by comparison."

"I heed thee not, varlet," said Captain Nazi. "For I darest not screw up the allegory. I art an actor first and foremost, and I believest the play's the thing. But I trow when this thing is over I'll boot your ass, Kevin."

"Bushwah," hooted Kevin. "You're full of prunes, and so is your allegory."

"I got the background material for this play right from the ruins of the University of Southern California, Kevin. I didn't swipe it from my betters like you, you dumb jigaboo."

95

"Boo, boo," said some of the girls.

"Let's keep the race question out of this," suggested Kevin. He ran, hopped up on the slightly raised stage. "Bad theater is bad theater, regardless of race."

"Toss him off," said the Spirit of a Steady Job, rising on one elbow and wiping blood from his mouth. "We have to get on with this. We haven't even stomped the Devil yet."

"Begone," Captain Nazi ordered the black actor.

"No, I'm here to discuss my objections to your play." He swung on Captain Nazi and knocked him over.

"Give us a chance to finish it before you start making criticisms," said the Spirit of a Steady Job.

Hecker hunkered to the left and got the last of the ropes cut away. The chain padlock was twisted around behind him, jammed into the small of his back.

"Hey, you stupid shine!" shouted a burly blond actor in the audience. "Stop knocking King Arthur around."

"Oh, it's the leader of the Bowery Boys Memorial Theater," said Kevin. "Shut up, you phony."

"Is this the spirit of free expression?" asked the Bowery Boy. "Let's all calm down now and let the good captain continue."

Two Negro actors hit him with rocks.

Captain Nazi shouted, "That, I woost, is the straw that breaks the conscience of the king." He got fully to his feet, kicked Kevin once in the stomach, and then flung himself into the audience.

The hundreds of young girls there were rising up rapidly, waving arms, clutching themselves in spasms of anguish, screaming, cheering. About fifty actors were brawling by the time Captain Nazi punched the head Bowery Boy.

"There it is," said Barbie. She was behind Hecker and helped him get the key into the padlock.

He shook free of ropes and chains and, taking the girl by the hand, ran from the rough amphitheater. In the woods, Barbie pulled to a stop and let go of him.

"I'm staying, Sergeant Hecker."

"You sure you want to?"

"No, but I will for a while anyway."

Hecker watched her for a few seconds. "You shouldn't."

"I guess I know." She turned away.

Hecker went on.

CHAPTER 13

He tumbled. Down a sharp hillside rich with interlocked palm trees and tangled vines. There were so many big scarlet-petaled flowers, Hecker could not move forward without scattering petals, grinding them to fragments. Glimpses he was catching of the old Wheelan Studios buildings' buff-painted plaster walls and red-tile roofs forming a great square fortress. But there seemed to be no passway to the place.

Hecker worked into the underbrush, in and around where there seemed to be no way of passing but always was, finally. Suddenly there was a wooden door in the jungle, masked almost completely by thick ferns and green brush. He touched at the door. It swung inward. A bare, tan arm knifed out, a hand caught his wrist and tugged.

"You're not as good at stalking as you could be." Jane

Kendry pulled him into a long, pastel-walled corridor. "I heard you a good five minutes away."

"I figured you were here." Hecker grinned at her. She'd discarded the blonde wig, and her auburn hair hung down. "You okay?"

"Yes. Yourself?" She quietly closed the door to the jungle, bolted it.

"Fine. What part of the studio is this?"

"The writers' building. That jungle out there isn't all Southern California gone to seed. The back lot, where they used to make jungle films, was there. This area gets left pretty much alone by scavengers."

"I met," Hecker told her, "Mama Lemon."

Jane walked away, further into the building. "Yes, she's the one who first showed me this all. How is she?"

"I don't know," admitted Hecker. "I ran into her and her group while I was searching for you. Then the Police Corps pulled a raid. I don't quite see why. They killed one guy, at least. That's not supposed to happen."

"But does." Jane entered a doorless office. "Maybe you've been out here, outside, too long." On top of a bright and undusty metal desk was a dictating/typing unit, compact and chromed. "An antique. From the late nineteen-seventies."

"What," asked Hecker, "happened to you back at Rancho Dos Passos?"

Jane was squinting at the two framed photographs on the wall—one of an actress unknown to either of them, and one of a plump man in an old-fashioned skydiving suit standing next to a brand-new 1980 hopper. "I'm not sure, exactly. I got very angry all of a sudden, felt like running, smashing things. There are times, I have to admit, when I've felt like that before. Usually I don't do anything about it." She faced him, her head slightly tilted and her smile quiet. "Nor do I have so much company. I don't recall hearing any voice telling me to break things and set fires. The impulses just popped up and I went ahead. Whatever it is Gadget Man has got, it's effective."

"How long did the spell, or whatever, last?"

She touched her tongue tip to her upper lip. "Oh, a good hour and a half. It slowed gradually, wore off. I stopped."

Hecker nodded. One of the room's high windows showed jungle and sunlight.

"I didn't come back to Dos Passos," said Jane, "for a couple of reasons. I knew the Army, the Police Corps, they'd all hit the suburb. And I wanted to get off by myself for a while." She looked away, toward a window showing the ruins of sound stages and the remnants of standing motion-picture sets. "You, Jim, didn't feel anything? You weren't compelled to riot."

"I felt a little extra anger, I guess. Not enough to want to smash somebody, something."

"You're a much steadier person," said Jane. "You know my record. You've probably talked to Rehab Center people."

"There was a guy named Weeman I talked to, yes. He offered to help you. He told me . . ." Hecker stopped, tugged at his mustache. "Except I just realized I don't trust Weeman."

"Dr. Weeman." Jane traced the line of her jaw with her finger. "He wasn't bad. He said he understood me. He didn't understand our cause, though."

"You and your father's cause."

"It's not only ours," said the girl. "We have thousands of people in the Republic of Southern California who sympathize with us. Only a small percent of the total population as yet, but we are going to topple the Junta eventually, Jim. The rest of the United States is still too screwed up to interfere, not for the next few years anyway." Jane folded her arms tight under her breasts. "You have a look in your eyes. You're not convinced."

"Are you?" asked Hecker. "All your raids, all your forays. You really believe they're aimed at gaining control of the government and setting up a better system?"

"You may have read a lot of files, background material on the Kendrys. You didn't grow up with my father. You don't understand him. His methods, his style."

"I tried to understand them in San Cabrito," said Hecker. "And understand what happened to Hash Sontag and the others."

"Your people did that to Hash."

Hecker watched the jungle.

"Okay," said Jane finally. "My father drinks sometimes now, a lot now. You have to know him, though, Jim. You have to know what he's lived, know about my mother. Then you could maybe . . ." After a moment Jane said, "We're quite near former Vice-president Westlake's Don't Tread On Me Electronic Dance Pavilion. We'll go there tonight and see what we can find out."

"Same is still hunting you."

"You, too, probably. Nobody knows we're heading for the dance pavilion except my adopted brother, Jack. I have a feeling Jack is okay and hiding someplace," said Jane. "As far as my father knows, I'm off on another of my rambles. You've stopped making any reports to the Social Wing, haven't you?"

"There hasn't, what with one thing and another, been much opportunity," said Hecker. "Seems safer not to. The

SW allows us to extemporize and do what the assignment calls for."

"Extemporize and do what the assignment calls for," repeated the girl, hugging herself tighter. "That's secured-living talk. Why do you have to be so stiff and quiet?"

Hecker rubbed his healing face wound, then scratched a spot on his back where one of Captain Nazi's actors had booted him. "We're both feeling a little ambiguous today."

"I don't agree."

"Look," said Hecker, "we can sleep together right now. You don't have to start an argument to get there."

Jane remained motionless for several seconds, then lowered her arms.

The red wind came swooping in all around them, hot and dry.

"Santa Anna wind," said Jane. She was walking naked past the First National Bank.

Across the street from her, in the South Seas, Hecker was relaxing against a grass shack. "We better get back inside."

"In a little while." The wind increased as twilight spread through the vast movie lot.

"You'll get all chapped." Hecker rose up, scratched his bare shoulder.

A wooden eagle blew off the city hall of Elm City and fell near Jane. She crossed the street, where dust was rising, and joined Hecker. "When I was a girl these winds used to scare me. Not now, though. Did they you?"

"No," said Hecker. Part of Greenwich Village blew over, and they had to sidetrack and dodge to miss being hit by the false front of a coffeehouse.

"You don't," observed Jane, "care to talk about your past much." She rested her palm on his back. The warm wind whipped her auburn hair.

"Or anybody's," he said. "Present company excepted."

"You did grow up around here?"

Palm leaves began to fall, like spears. "Yes, more or less. Up in Santa Barbara."

"Oh? It's pretty there still. We raided there once."

Half of a saloon door came cartwheeling along the street, and Hecker pulled Jane out of its way. "Yes, it is. Most parts."

"What about your family?"

The hot Santa Anna wind tore the last piece of ginger-bread from the white Nob Hill mansion next to them. "We're not a large group, like the Kendrys."

"Jim, come on. I'm legitimately curious."

Hecker said, "Well, my mother was on the staff of some-thing called the Poverty Aid Experiment. Most of the time I knew her anyway. She died some twenty years ago. In Santa Barbara, on the edges. Where the poverty she was supposed to be aiding was. Natural causes."

"Your father?"

Hecker shrugged, ducked away from a falling piece of the Colosseum. "I never met him. She had some friends in the hall of records there, and they were able to fake a few things. Hecker was actually her maiden name, though it doesn't say that on my file. As for the James Xavier part, I never found out where that came from."

"Xavier is a saint's name."

"Maybe my father was a holy man."

"Does it," asked Jane, "bother you not knowing?"

"No," said Hecker. "Well, yes. *Then* it did."

Jane began a smile that turned into a pleased laugh.

"I love you, James Xavier Hecker. For what that's worth."

Hecker laughed back. "That's good. That's fine." Egypt was blowing away behind them, and he caught up the girl and carried her back inside one of the real buildings.

CHAPTER 14

The glass pavilion was filled with neon flags. They flashed red, white, and blue all around and overhead, interrupted by stars and night clouds showing above the great glass, squared dome. Undulating around the upper walls, in multicolored translux, was the name DON'T TREAD ON ME DANCE PAVILION. Below the name, in electric cross-stitch, pulsed a sign saying: YOUR HOST, NATHAN E. WESTLAKE, FORMER VICE-PRESIDENT OF THE UNITED STATES OF AMERICA. On pedestals at twice eye level were android replicas of the past Presidents of the United States. Just inside the wide doorway of the glass pavilion, his back to the three hundred dancing patrons, was a small, black man in a powdered wig and buckskin suit. "Welcome to the Don't Tread on Me," he said as Hecker and Jane entered.

"Good evening," said Hecker.

"I am," said the black man, "Ralph E. Prickens. If you're

fans of American history, you may remember me as the first Negro Secretary of Defense."

"Didn't your policies," said Jane, who'd borrowed a dark wig from the abandoned movie-studio costume room, "lead to . . ."

"The ultimate collapse of the United States Government," said Prickens. "It's nice to be remembered."

"There was," added Hecker, talking above the music, "the SFX scandal, too."

"Yes," said the Negro, touching his dusted wig. "A high point in my career, the SFX scandal."

"Was the SFX a fighter plane or a missile?" asked Jane. "I don't recall."

"Nobody was ever sure," said Prickens. "Which made for part of the scandal. It was glorious in our nation's capital in those days, when we still had a nation."

"Who," asked Hecker, his hand on Jane's arm lightly, "are you dressed as, Mr. Secretary?"

"Guess."

"The wig is George Washington," said Jane and got a pleased nod. "The buckskin is Daniel Boone."

"To be eclectic and patriotic is very satisfying," said Prickens, his head bobbing pleasantly. "When you tire of dancing, I'll show you my Museum of Historical American Weaponry. You two seem mature enough to appreciate the American past at its best."

There was a ratcheting crash far across the pavilion. Hecker pointed. "President Hoover just fell off his pedestal."

Prickens patted his wig and grinned. "Yes, he's programed to do that. Customers get bored seeing the andies just dance and make speeches."

"We've heard a lot about, though we've never been

here before, the former Vice-president," said Jane. "Is there any chance of getting a glimpse of Mr. Westlake himself?"

"Up on the bandstand touching his toes," said the black man. "It's a new dance step the VP is working out. See him there? Touch your left toe, jump up, snap your fingers, touch your right toe, pat your fanny, snap your fingers, walk like a duck."

The bandstand in the Don't Tread on Me was mounted on four eagle-topped flagpoles, filled with electronic musicians dressed like the Union Army. Former Vice-president Westlake, his familiar cigar in his mouth, was dancing in front of the Fender bass section, dressed as Abraham Lincoln. He lost his stovepipe hat in the midst of a frantic duck walk and swung off the high platform, slid down a pole. On the red, white, and blue mosaic dance floor he shrugged his Lincoln shawl off his shoulders and toweled it back and forth across his buttocks.

"He can relax more here than he did in the White House," said Prickens. "There he was too hampered and pressured." He smiled suddenly at Hecker and Jane. "You don't really want to dance now. Come and see my museum first off. I'll fetch the Vice-president, and you can shake his hand, and he might give you one of his souvenir cigars."

They followed the former Secretary of Defense, zigzag, through the dancers, most of whom looked young and untroubled. Highlights from the life of Benjamin Franklin were carved on the door of the Museum of Historical American Weaponry. It was a dome too, half as large as the dance pavilion. The weapons—muskets, cannons, M-16s, bazookas, flintlocks, flame throwers, grenades, and things not easily identifiable—were in great heaps on the mosaic floor.

"I haven't systematized this wealth of stuff yet," admitted Prickens. He removed his powdered wig and exhaled. "To me the biggest thrill is in the collecting. Cataloguing and sorting are enervating. Over in that area I have my planes. Bombers, fighters. I've been exceptionally lucky on warplanes lately. Got my hands on some truly nice items." He gestured at a half-dozen battered airplanes that formed a vast winged heap against a far wall. Two of the planes were upside down. Instruments and wires hung down out of the open cockpit of one. "Come over and get a closer glimpse."

"Impressive," said Hecker as they drew closer to the mound of airships.

Up and out of the cockpit of an ancient World War II fighter plane emerged a lean gray man in a seamless gray suit. "Snared again," he said. It was Second Lieutenant Same with a bright pistol, the newest weapon in the museum, in his lean right hand.

"We got them good," said Prickens. "I spotted them right off."

"What are you up to, Same?" Hecker asked.

Second Lieutenant Same smiled, his face remaining sad. "Let me admit," he said, swinging out of the ship, "my interest in Miss Kendry is more than an expression of interest on the part of Manipulation Council."

"I figured," said Hecker.

"Exactly," said Same. "I serve a variety of causes. The riot sponsors are among those I work for. Questioning Miss Kendry will help me serve two masters, the riot-makers and Manipulation Council. As will eliminating her."

"Did you follow us here somehow?" Jane took Hecker's hand, watching Same. "Who told you we'd come here?"

Same dropped from the warplane to the floor. "An awkward boy named Jack. I acquired him after your family doings. He was the only one who seemed to know."

Jane moved sideways and ahead, hit Same across the mouth with her fist.

Second Lieutenant Same said, "It's sometimes valuable to work out frustrations physically."

Prickens grabbed the girl, warning, "Calm yourself, miss."

"The boy managed to slip away while being escorted to a rural detention station," said Same. "An aggressive little misfit."

"They seemed to like the dancing," said former Vice-president Westlake, who had come into the weapons dome while Jane was swinging on Same. "That Latin touch at the finish drew a nice round of applause. Is this them?"

"I want," said the second lieutenant, "to find out what the girl knows and whom she's told about it. I want to find out what the social worker knows and whom he's told about it."

Westlake's double-chinned face was still deeply pink from the exertion of dancing. "Did you bring your own interrogation equipment? Ralph's is always going on the fritz. Most of it is outmoded junk from the war with Brazil."

"I can't keep every single damn thing around here shipshape," said Prickens.

Smiling sadly, Second Lieutenant Same reached behind him for a small, pebbled tan case. "I always use my own."

Westlake started a fresh cigar going. "Once Swingle

takes over, we won't have to worry about outmoded equipment."

"Don't mention his name," said Same, his free hand setting the case on a pile of rifles.

"Whose name? Swingle's?" asked Westlake. "One thing I learned in nearly eight long years in the White House, Same, is that it really doesn't matter what you say in front of expendable people."

Prickens let go of Jane, moved closer to Same's interrogation case. He said, powdered wig in hand, "Let's not squabble in front of company."

Hecker pushed Jane aside, said, "Take cover." He kicked Prickens' wig out of his hand and it sailed, hard, into Same's face.

The second lieutenant's blaster crackled, cutting a rut across the side of a Patton tank.

Hecker then caught both ends of the Vice-president's shawl, tugged with alternate motions, and spun Westlake into Prickens. The two men lost balance and toppled into Second Lieutenant Same, who went over backwards and shot a square of blue glass out of the dome high above.

Hecker drew his own pistol and sent a warning blast at the tangle of men. He vaulted a pile of gasmasks and airplane helmets and found Jane. The slender girl was throwing dud hand grenades in the direction of Same. "Let's leave," Hecker suggested.

They swung up a bazooka and used it as a ram to shatter out a section of the glass wall of the museum dome. Hecker fired again over his shoulder as Same, looking both sad and grim, got himself righted and ready to shoot.

There was a fifty-yard stretch of empty field, high grass,

behind the dome. Hecker and Jane crashed out, ran across it before Second Lieutenant Same could make his way through the souvenirs and reach the shattered place in the wall.

There was an acre of ornamental forest next, then a few small beach cottages. In front of the second darkened house a hover scooter was parked. "Hold them off," said Jane, "until I can job this thing."

"No sign of anybody yet."

Jane picked the lock over the starting compartment of the two-seat scooter and had the machine going before the lights of the cottage came on full.

CHAPTER 15

The fog began to thin and the water to lighten. Jane turned away from Hecker, and the borrowed gray blanket slipped off her shoulders. Hecker sat up, flexed, rubbed his head. A breakfast fire had started up nearby. Hecker sat watching the ocean, then studied the scatter of people camped on this stretch of unsecured beach.

A Mexican girl in a cast-off Chinese Commando field jacket cocked a hand at him and mouthed the word *coffee*. Hecker gestured *yes*, stood.

Jane moaned once, sat up full awake. "Morning," she said.

"Want some coffee?" Hecker knelt, rested his palm on the back of her neck.

"Sure."

Hecker walked across the cold sand to the dark girl. "Spare two cups?"

"Yeah, easy. You know Marsloff, don't you?" When Hecker nodded she said, "He's parked near that tumble-down penny arcade up the beach. He noticed you when he arrived last night. He says if you want a ride any-where, you and Jane, ask him. Even if you don't, step over and say hello."

With Jane again, Hecker asked, "Can we trust Mar-sloff?"

"Yes." Jane took a mug of hot coffee from him.

"He seems to be up the beach, offering us a lift."

"We're still twenty miles from Swingleton," said the long girl. "It was a good idea to ditch the borrowed scooter where we did, but we can use new transporta-tion."

"Swingle, the man Westlake mentioned, still lives there?"

"Far as I know." Jane warmed her chin against the cup. "Erwin LeBeck Swingle. He was supposed to be the second richest man in the country, back when there was still a functioning United States. It must be two or three decades ago he bought up most of the Anaheim Sector and turned it into a model city for older people."

"I've heard of him, too. He has to be about ninety years old." Hecker drank some of his strong coffee. "He is the kind of guy who could be tied in with Westlake and his patriotic pavilion."

"I wonder if Swingle is at the top of the riotmakers."

"You mean, could Swingle be the Gadget Man?"

"Sure, he is," said Marsloff, who trotted up to them now. "He's a gadget man."

"Not *a. The.*" Hecker shook hands with the big shaggy man.

116

"That I don't know," said Marsloff. "Swingle is a gadget freak, though. Every once in a while my partner, Percher comes up with something new in the way of gadget kicks. We go down to Swingleton and sell the thing to one of old Swingle's reps. I'd estimate there are dozens of gadget freaks who supply him."

Hecker asked, "Who do you contact in Swingleton?"

"Never the old man himself. Him we've never seen." Marsloff sniffed and started backing toward the girl with the coffee, still talking. "Swingle we have never met. There are a couple people work there that we deal with." The Mexican girl put a cup of coffee in his hairy hand, and he kissed her cheek before trotting again to Hecker and Jane. "I can give you their names if you need them."

Hecker massaged his knuckles. "Could Percher work up something in the way of a gadget? It doesn't have to be that original. Jane and I have to get inside Swingleton, near to Swingle. I want something we can use as a passport."

"You're in luck." Marsloff drank down his coffee. "Because Percher is awake today, and he was telling me he's in a creative mood. All we got to do is find him."

"He's not with you?" asked Jane.

"The little guy took off at dawn on a motorbike," said Marsloff. "He's got friends and customers around here. We can go looking for him if it's a rush."

"It's a rush," Jane told him.

The beautiful girl in the tailored overalls said, "Or perhaps you know someone who's taking an ocean trip." She gestured at a shelf holding a gift basket of potatoes with a bon voyage ribbon.

The produce stand was at the entrance of the hundred-

117

acre farm Marsloff had brought them to. It was built of raw wood and had real glass windows. Out in the fields beyond, Marsloff was asking questions. "Everything is potatoes," observed Jane.

The pretty brunette sighed. "We didn't have any luck with our other crops. A gift box of individually wrapped potatoes isn't as impressive as bing cherries or satsuma plums, but the bugs and some kind of little white stuff killed all our fruit. And the birds, they're really awful."

"You all here belong to some movement?" asked Hecker. "The Agrarians, isn't it?"

"That's correct, yes," said the pretty girl. "We believe the only way to get in tune with the real meaning of the world is to get out and be close to the earth, the land. You've probably never heard of an author named Candide, but he had the same notion many centuries ago. Cultivate your garden, he admonished. So all of us kids in the Agrarians have gotten right out here and tilled the soil and sown the seeds and reaped the harvest."

"Which was potatoes this year," said Hecker.

"We don't exactly have a green thumb yet," admitted the girl. "Not at this particular farm anyhow. Some of the kids in other locations have had really swell luck."

"Who owns this farm?"

"Betsy Parkinson's father bought it for us. He's the cemetery-module tycoon from Palos Verdes, as you probably well know." The girl absently polished a jar of potato conserve with the sleeve of her silk blouse. "Betsy doesn't even like to come here any more, though."

"Why is that?" asked Jane. Marsloff had stopped talking to people in the fields and was striding back.

"Because of the pickets," the girl told them. "They're not supposed to picket us at all. But if you call the Police

Corps they come and shoot them, and some of us don't like that. I don't know if you've ever seen a dead person, but it's very unpleasant. These pickets are Mexican-Americans."

Marsloff came into the stand. "That little rascal," he said. "Percher's gone down to the town of Gomez, about five miles from here, to visit a hardware store. You know, a place that caters to gadget freaks. We'll catch him there."

"This is Gomez," announced Marsloff, hitting the brakes on his land truck.

The town was one block long, adobe and dust. The heat of the afternoon sizzled in the air, and dogs sprawled in deathlike positions in rectangles of shade. In front of the Veterans of the Chinese Invasion hall a seventy-year-old man in tennis shorts was sipping an orange drink.

Hecker and Jane trailed Marsloff across the dry, dusty street and up the wooden steps of the Anmar Brothers Hardware Store. Tiny gray bugs hovered in the hot air at eye level. Inside the small store it was chill and filled with motorized noise. "The brothers are air-conditioning freaks," explained Marsloff. He gestured with a hairy arm at the two-dozen large electric fans humming all around the hardware store.

"And where's Percher?" asked Hecker.

"The real hardware store, the gadget-freak hangout, is down below," said Marsloff. "They figure nobody will look under a hardware store for a hardware store."

Behind a wood counter that was gray with age slouched one of the Anmar brothers. He was a middle-aged man, tall and sloped. On the bib of his tartan overalls was pinned a tag reading: HI, I'M FRANK ANMAR. He was listening to a freckled, grease-spotted young man in a buff-colored jumpsuit. Finally Anmar said, "Well, no wonder."

"What do you mean, 'no wonder'?" asked the burly customer. He had been drawing a diagram on a pad with a yellow electric pencil.

"He's got them on upside down." Anmar titled and poked at the drawing.

"Upside down?"

"Yeah. Which is the reason why you got this problem now."

"Well, but he said they were right side up. He's in the business, after all."

Anmar nodded with sympathy. "He's the fellow has a brother-in-law in the synthetic-lumber business up in the Fresno Sector, isn't he?"

"Well, yes."

"Upside down."

"Now, well, what am I going to do? I already paid him the $1000. If they're all upside down. I mean, what would you suggest, Frank?"

"I'm Bill. Wearing Frank's overalls today," said the Anmar brother. "Only thing I'd recommend to do is take them down."

"Take them down?"

"Yes. Then put them back up. Right side up."

"Oh, boy."

Marsloff made a sign at Bill Anmar, finger exercises in the air. The proprietor winked quickly, sloped more and reached under the counter. "Better to do it now than after the season," he told his customer.

"Back here behind the ladders," said Marsloff.

Out of sight of the counter stood a pile of unfinished

near-wood stepladders, with room enough between them and the wall to pass. Marsloff squeezed behind the ladders. Hecker and Jane followed. A narrow doorway had slid open in the old wooden wall, and beyond it was a stairway. Down below the store, through a wood-walled tunnel, were interconnected caverns. Each man-made cavern was large and high-ceilinged, reinforced with metal arches and beams. Unshaded light globes and dusty light strips glowed at infrequent spots. Water had dripped down in various places, and there were small pools and mildew splotches over the wood-plank flooring.

The first cavern was empty except for a lean light-haired man in a fog-colored suit. He sat on a stool, mid-room, with a blaster rifle resting on his thin lap. "Ah, there, Marsloff," he said.

"Seen my partner?" asked Marsloff. "This is Jane Kendry and Jim Hecker. This is Kenneth R. Eiffeler."

Eiffeler puckered his mouth. He had a mustache similar to Hecker's, only pale blond. "Ah, the well-known resistance leader. I'm in complete sympathy with your cause, Miss Kendry, though devoted to a more profitable and less dangerous one myself."

"We're anxious," said Jane, "to locate Percher."

A chalk-colored girl, thin and silent, had appeared in the arched entrance of one of the other caverns. "My mistress," said Eiffeler. "Maisie Macmillan. She's as fond of all this hardware as I am." He bounced off his stool. "Actually, I'd originally intended this as a museum. A tribute to industry and technology. I couldn't get funding, however."

"Who would fund this crud?" asked Maisie. Her voice seemed to come not from her but from the cavern she had left.

"She actually loves the stuff but is shy with strangers."

"The stuff is crud. The people too droopy to bother with." She shrugged, barely moving.

"Percher is indeed here. Maisie will guide you, like a Virgil in drag, right to him," said Eiffeler. "I think he's using one of the workshops."

"And won't clean up the mess after." Maisie gestured to the three.

"Do you," Hecker asked Eiffeler, who was remounting his stool, "know anything about Gadget Man?"

"He never heard of him," said Maisie. "Come on."

"What about Erwin LeBeck Swingle?" persisted Hecker.

"He's on my customer list," said Eiffeler. "I have three lists actually: A, B, and C. Swingle's on A. He buys a lot of assorted stuff."

"Crud."

"He once purchased a Santa Fe railroad club car from me."

"We still got the rest of the lousy train stored here," said Maisie. "It's a bitch to dust."

"I gambled on the train," said Eiffeler. "The guy who offered it wanted to sell it as a set. I wasn't sure how many of our gadget freaks would want a gadget that big."

Maisie said, "Come on, Marsloff. We'll find your droopy partner."

"I love that woman," Eiffeler said. "Though if it were not for her, I'd have the largest collection of gadgets in the Republic of Southern California."

The next cavern was devoted to simple electric shocks. The customers were seated around card tables and crates. Enjoying joy buzzers, faulty wiring, gimmicked appliances. A compact blond young man was off in a corner being playfully throttled by a vacuum cleaner. A plump Negro girl was dancing with a pinball machine. Behind curtains, in candlelit alcoves, more complicated acts were being performed. Involving electrified fence wire, vibrator lounge chairs, exercise bikes, under-age girls. The cavern rang with electric buzzings and hummings, cries of pleasure, moans of pain, chuckles, rattling. A bald man carrying a bureau drawer full of electric mixers and battery-powered eggbeaters tripped over a young couple who were hugging in an ice-cube machine. There was more clatter.

"Percher's not here," said Maisie, leading them through.

"Obviously," said Marsloff. "These are second-balcony types. Percher is a box seat."

The next cavern was quiet and well lit. Couples sat on old room group furniture, and there was no sign of any gadgetry.

"What's this one devoted to?" Jane asked.

"Microminiaturization gadget freaks," explained Marsloff. "They're all getting excited, but the gadgets are too small to see."

A handsome matron, with a tennis-court tan, yelped with glee to the left of the way they were passing. A ruddy-cheeked, middle-aged man was bent over, gently tapping at the floor with his palms. "Don't step on it," he cautioned. "It fell off."

"Maybe he had it on upside down," Jane said to Hecker.

The cavern that followed looked much like the Prickens museum. It was all war gadgets, guns and flame throwers, and old planes. Enjoying themselves here, wired in or merely cavorting, were mostly retired RSC

Army officers and their high-school drum-majorette companions.

There was also a cavern where you could be electrically and mechanically stimulated while reclining in a fleet of old school buses. And then a cavern where several people sat and just watched a rotating display of exciting gadgets: self-winding vinyl shavers, laminated automatic mattress inflaters, combination spectrometer-tachometers, Old West-style laser guns, disposable artificial epoxy kidneys, solid-state microwave oscillators in decorator colors, electroluminescent diodes in personalized carrying cases, solar-powered nose-hair clippers, princess-style videophones, geodesic teakettles, injection-molded garlic presses, manually operated cherrystoners, alligator-finished episcopes, magnetostriction ultrasonic generators on patio stands, self-turning kaleidoscopes, robot flatirons, vestpocket bronchoscopes, paisley-surfaced binnacles, miniaturized vacuum cleaners, musical abacuses.

Maisie shook her head briefly. "What a way to make a living." She ushered them into a thin corridor that smelled of lubricating oil and old land-car polishing rags. Knocking once on a real wood door, she said, "He's in there, diddling around," and left them.

Percher was small, freckled over with pale-brown freckles. He had on a smock made from a secondhand dress shirt. "Hey, Marsloff," he grinned, looking up from the metallic table. "Hey, Jane." He frowned at Hecker, then grinned. "You have a nice mustache and a nice head of hair, buddy. My hair never stays combed." This was true. "How I got into gadgetry in the first place was fooling with electric combs and trying to get my cowlick to lie flat. I turned a fine-tooth comb on too high and gave myself the most exquisite shock I'd ever experienced up to that moment. Hey, Marsloff, why are you here? Is there trouble?"

"There's always trouble someplace," answered his partner. "This is Jane Kendry's friend I told you about. Jim Hecker. He'll explain."

"We want," said Hecker, "to get into Swingleton. To see Swingle."

"Hey, okay. This guy is trustworthy, isn't he, Jane?"

"Yes, he's fine," she said.

"Hey, that's good," said Percher. "You like him. I can tell. It's good to relate to people. To relate to a guy with a nice mustache and a nice head of hair is good for you, Jane. My problem is I can't relate to people as well as to inanimate things. It's a mild form of necrophilia."

"A psychiatrist told him," put in Marsloff.

"It was an android psychiatrist," said Percher. "So I believed him. He didn't cure me, but he made explaining my obsession easier."

"Do you have some new gadget we can borrow?" Jane asked.

"To use as a decoy, a passport to get inside Swingle's place," said Hecker.

"Hey, an electronic Trojan Horse." Percher grinned. "I just invented something. It might be terrific for you."

"We can borrow it?"

"Hey, Jane, you can keep it forever," said Percher.

125

CHAPTER 16

Marsloff's land truck got ten feet past the giant orange and stopped, with one last string of barking and ratcheting. "Out of fuel," said Marsloff, puzzled. "I had half a tank when we left Gomez."

Hecker stretched awake in the passenger seat, noticed through the porthole window that Jane was still stretched out and asleep on a pile of sacking in the closed back of the truck. He said, "We passed an open fuel station about six blocks back. I'll go for some."

Marsloff tapped a big finger against the fuel gauge. "I guess you should, though there may be something else wrong. I'll fiddle around here. Too bad that little rascal Percher stayed at the hardware store. He's got a great gift for repairs."

The two men swung out of opposite sides of the truck cab and dropped to the night pavement. The orange next to them was the size of a cottage, made of corrugated metal. HONEST RALPH'S JUICE TOWN was lettered over its shuttered serving window, and the dull silvery color of the metal was showing through the orange paint. "Let Jane rest," Hecker said.

The streets were better lighted the nearer Hecker got to the center of town. He walked by a tin orange that was still in business. RIORITA BEACH'S FINEST JUICE BAR! it announced in citrus-colored light strips. The juice stand's only customers were two female impersonators sharing a limeade.

Hecker was still a good half block from Bozo's All-Nite Gas Stop when Rollo and Milo Kendry appeared on each side of him.

"Say, look at this," said Milo, punching Hecker in the spine. "It's sure enough Cousin Jim. How're you?"

"Excellent," said Hecker.

Rollo nuzzled his ringleted head against Hecker's shoulder and pulled at his ear. "This is one of those happy coincidences you hear about, ain't it, Milo?"

"It's a bugger all right," said the other big Kendry boy. "We're on the town, Cousin Jim. Now, woowee, you can up and join us."

"No, thanks, Milo."

Rollo caught Hecker under the arms and danced him around on the sidewalk. "Don't spoil our fine times, Cousin Jim." He spun free of Hecker, clogged alone on the cracked cement. "We're tired and don't like for anyone to act surly with us."

"We been looking," explained Milo, "for Jane. Jess is really worrying and grieving over her. Have you seen her, Cousin Jim?"

"Not since San Cabrito."

"Wasn't that a mess?" asked Milo. "This poor pea-brained rube here spoiled that raid for sure."

128

"Did not either," said Rollo. "You ought to stop always being so highly critical all the time."

They were opposite the fuel station now. Hecker said, "I have some stuff to take care of, boys. You go on and have fun."

"Won't be no fun if you abandon us," said Rollo. He grabbed Hecker's arm hard. "You come on now. We're making up a theater party."

Milo took his other arm. "You'll have a real swell time, Cousin Jim. Our favorite actor is putting on a special show at the Riorita Beach Rivoli Playhouse." He strained, and the two Kendrys lifted Hecker up. "It is no less than Captain Nazi in person."

Hecker said as he was carried through the night, "I've already seen it."

"A work of art you can sit through twice. Don't be a thick-witted cluck like Milo."

They jostled Hecker down an alley and around a brick corner and up to the box office.

The audience tonight was mixed. Three hundred young girls and about two hundred men, a great many of them Kendrys and Kendry associates. Milo selected three seats close to the stage of the ramshackle but once ornate theater. He threw the occupants of the seats onto the Arabic aisle rug. "Park your ass, Cousin Jim," he suggested. "We missed the prologue, looks like."

He slammed Hecker into the middle seat of three, took the aisle seat, clapped his big hands together in happy anticipation.

"Move your outsize oafish feet," said Rollo. He stomped over Milo's legs, tripped on Hecker, and clumped down into the last empty chair.

A fragile young Chinese girl was next to him. "You

129

just dropped your fat butt on my opera glasses," she told Rollo.

Rollo snorted, frowned. "You hadn't ought to talk that way, miss." He reached under himself and extracted the small pair of binoculars. "What a man likes in a girl is a certain sweet reserve. Nobody likes a badmouth."

"Bushwah." The girl snatched her glasses off his palm.

"Oh," chuckled Rollo. "You're being kittenish. I get it. Well, save your time, miss. I'm spoken for."

"Shut your big flabby bazoon," whispered Milo. "I want to hear the play." He leaned in front of Hecker and wrapped Rollo on the ear. "Don't be a lousy dilettante."

The curtain, all peacock designs and tropical flowers, had opened and revealed Captain Nazi alone in a shabby saloon. He wore the top half of a suit of gilded armor and was leaning at the bar meditatively.

"What's the name of tonight's allegory?" Milo asked Rollo.

"I forget."

"It's entitled," said the pretty Chinese teen-ager, "*Sir Galahad's Bar and Grill.* Now shut the heck up."

"Hush yourself, miss," warned Rollo. "Remember what I said about foul talk from the lips of ladies."

"Bushwah."

Captain Nazi turned toward the audience, spread his arms out at his side, reclined against the bar. "What in the hell is life all about?"

The bartender wandered in and tied on his dirty apron. "Search me. What'll it be?"

"A beaker of froth from the wine-dark sea," said Captain Nazi. "A cool draught of warm spring."

"We don't serve fancy mixed drinks here."

"O gods who transcribe man's fate in great scrolls,

130

what hast thee in mind for your humble servant? Aye, and forthwith I am weary, footsore, and fancy free. I have been on yon quest for lo these many years. Zounds, where is the Holy Grail?"

"We ain't got that either," said the bartender. "How about a beer."

"Let me talk to the manager."

"Ah, no, alas, none may do that, sire," replied the bartender. "He is a man of infinite mysteriousness and mystification. He moves on the winds of the world, and his ways are dark and arcane." He wiped the bar top. "I wouldn't stay here myself except I've built up so much in retirement pay."

"Ah, poor fool," shouted Captain Nazi. "A slave to routine, a clock puncher."

"Don't go calling me a clock puncher."

Hecker sat up some. He noticed Kevin, the black actor who'd help start the frumus in the outdoor theater, was sitting two rows directly in front of him.

"What, O dark gods, am I to do?" Captain Nazi demanded of the ceiling.

"Stomp him," suggested the Chinese girl.

Hecker cupped his hands to his mouth. "He'd rather kiss him."

Captain Nazi lowered his eyes from above and scowled at the audience. He was grimacing directly at Kevin, who shifted in his seat. "What course, O ye gads of fair play, am I to follow. What primrose path must I tread? Wouldst I engage in mortal combat?"

"Why not get engaged, you fairies!" called Hecker.

"Cousin Jim, restrain yourself." Rollo elbowed him.

"Stomp him, stomp him," cried out a hundred intense girls.

131

Captain Nazi strode to the fluttering footlights. "Listen, Kevin, I know that's you. That rotten ofay voice you're putting on doesn't fool me a bit. We have a truce, remember, you benighted pickaninny." He rubbed at his eyepatch with an angry fist.

"I had," shouted Kevin, rising, "nothing to do with this latest in a long line of critical appraisals of your theater. However, I must admit I agree with it."

"You shut up," called the bartender.

"No, *you* shut up," said Kevin.

"Bunch of fruitcakes," said Hecker, head low. He jumped up suddenly and stepped down hard on Milo's feet. Milo screamed and jumped. Hecker ducked in front of him and landed in the aisle. Before Rollo could reach him, Hecker spun Milo into him. Then he chucked Milo back and into Kevin, who was just hitting the aisle on his way toward Captain Nazi and the stage.

"You guys are asking for it," warned Captain Nazi. He leaped from the stage.

Hecker about-faced, ran for the rear exit. He got halfway there when four Kendrys sprang up to block him. Hecker bicycled abruptly, climbed up to the seat tops and went tightrope fashion from chair back to chair back. He reached the next aisle, punched the one Kendry there and shouldered to the exit door. A hundred-man brawl was, as Hecker'd hoped, welling up behind him.

He used alleys and side streets, circling, running hard. He made it to the stalled land truck in ten minutes. All its doors that could be opened were open. Marsloff was on his face in the gravel in front of the abandoned tin orange.

Jane was gone.

CHAPTER 17

Beside the giant orange someone said, "James Xavier Hecker."

Hecker lifted his knee from the gravel beside the unconscious Marsloff. Slowly he moved his right hand toward his shoulder holster. "Yes?"

"Cut out the suspicious-acting crap," said a young voice. "Get Marsloff back here out of sight in case some more of the Kendrys come looking for you."

"Jack?" Hecker had determined Marsloff was not seriously hurt. He hauled the big shaggy man over into the deep shadows alongside the rusted juice stand.

"Exactly who it is," said the small out-of-kilter young man. "Adopted brother of Jane Kendry. Escape artist par excellence. That's a foreign phrase meaning 'damn good.'"

"The Kendrys took Jane?"

"Yes."

"Where'd they take her?"

"An orange crush to go," murmured Marsloff, half awake.

Jack said, "The Kendrys have had scouts trailing you since that dumb dance pavilion. They've been waiting for a chance to grab Jane. Jess is angry, mad all the time now. He wants Jane back by his side."

Marsloff tried to elbow to a sitting position. "They drilled a couple holes in my fuel tank."

"They sure did," said Jack. "While you were cavorting at that bordello for hardware freaks. Milo and Rollo were going to keep you out of the way, James, till Jane was grabbed. Then knock you on the head and dump you somewhere. I been trailing them by motorbike and foot since they took off after you and Jane." Jack's thin face had bruises on it, partly healed gashes.

"How'd they pick up our trail?" asked Hecker.

"I'm afraid I told them the basic details," said the frail boy. "After I eluded those nitwits Second Lieutenant Same had turned me over to, I headed back for the Kendry camp. Too late to meet Jane and you. Right on time to feel Jess's wrath." He massaged his ribs. "When I was up and around, I lit out after them. To see what they'd do, warn Jane if I could."

"Hit me on the head," said Marsloff, pointing to his shaggy head. "A bunch of them."

"Do you," Hecker asked the boy, "know where Jane is being taken?"

Jack said, "They have a couple of unsettled and unsecured sites in this area. Jess Kendry favors that old abandoned oceanography park area a ways down the coast. It was called Fish/Utopia! and had seafood restaurants, whale in a tank, dolphins in panel-discussion

134

groups, fun for all. Bring the whole family. Closed down ten years ago, all the fish are dead. Nobody goes there."

"Okay. And the other place they might have headed?"

"Up in the hills, north of here. Stuntville, old authentic western town used in motion pictures and television. Cowboys, fights in saloons. Went broke."

"You think the beach place is most likely?"

"I think Jess favors it, yes."

"That shouldn't be more than five miles from here."

"Four and a half," said Jack.

"Now I know how Percher feels." Marsloff hid his head in his hands for a while.

Hecker said, "I'll go and talk to Jess."

"He was making like you stole Jane against her will," said the boy. "He might possibly have you slaughtered."

"He might."

"Wait until I stop being woozy," offered Marsloff, "and we'll get the truck fixed for the trip. You and me can tackle the Kendry stronghold together and see about Jane. Talk to Jess, who's acting awfully odd lately. Beat up a few guys if we have to."

"No," Hecker told him. "I'll go now, alone."

Jack smiled from the shadows. "You like Jane. She's important to you. You can't abide her suddenly going out of your life. I favor that, James. You can borrow my motorbike."

"You and Marsloff aren't going to be safe around here," said Hecker. "There are still angry Kendrys roaming the town looking for me."

"I know," said Jack, "a few people here. People who believe in Jane but not necessarily in some of the other Kendrys. Marsloff and I can be put up safely overnight. Kendrys like Milo and Rollo are restless. They won't stay around here playing at being a search party too long."

"Okay," said Hecker. "I'll accept the offer of the bike."

"It's a practically new bike," Jack explained. "I swiped it in front of a theological seminary near San Cabrito. Belonged to a young and active bishop."

"I'll use it only for good works," said Hecker.

The ocean had broken into the seafront remains of the aquatic park. Ornamental piers were half under water, pools of oily sea splotched the walkways. A great stuffed whale was on its back on a causeway, its underbelly shredded away and tufts of plastic excelsior around the gape. A seaside restaurant, once named The Cabin Boy, had crumbled in on itself. It had been an intricacy of imitation adobe arches and tile roofs, and now it was too many arches and not enough roofs.

Hecker had approached the place along the beach and was crouched in the scrub brush next to a concrete wall that had Fish/Utopia! painted on it in two-foot-high *sans serif* letters. Beneath this, almost weathered away, was printed: 6,526,000 HAPPY PEOPLE HAVE VISITED US . . . WELCOME!

The beach was narrow, a few feet of gritty sand at its widest. The darkness hung humid, and the stars were lost behind a gray haze. Up to Hecker's left, a quarter of a mile away, a few cook fires burned. He got himself a handhold in the pitted wall and went up and over. He landed in marshy weeds on the main street of a fishing village. AUTHENTIC PORTUGUESE WHALING TOWN said a tarnished plate on the nearest low stone building. ADMISSION ONE DOLLAR. The admitting turnstile had sunk into the softened ground, and only its four-pronged top showed above ground. There were still a few androids inhabiting the village, worn down and broken. A thin fisherman in the doorway of a stone house, leaning cockeyed. A blind beggar boy flat on his back in front of Manuel Do Pico's Authentic Restaurant. At the end of the street an old woman android, bent and in a body-length cloak and a hood. Hecker brushed against her and she whirred for a few seconds, told three rosary beads on the chain in her aged hands, and subsided.

Hecker kept in shadow and worked through the lanes of Fish/Utopia!, moving toward the fires and the now perceptible sounds of people. A seascape fell out of the Fish/Art Gallery as he passed and it skidded under his feet. Hecker dodged, then went on tiptoe to thread his way through the mounds of seashells in front of a ruined souvenir shop. Hundreds of broken ashtrays, announcing, now in fragments, WELCOME TO SOUTHERN CALIFORNIA!

A large two-story building was still standing in good shape, and Hecker cut through it. The door lettering said it had been the Sea Life Museum. There were scores of empty glass tanks around the big main room, nothing but dry seaweed in the bottom of them. The room was a full two stories high. Three flat skylights made its roof. The haze was thinning, shredding, and a few stars showed, and faint moonlight.

When Hecker was in midroom the lights inside an enormous water tank beside him sprang on. There was a tapping at the glass. Inside the tank, which was filled with fresh sea water, was a very old dolphin. The floor of his tank was a mingling of pipes and conduits, dials and switches, the control panel of a compact waterproof computer. The old dolphin grinned at Hecker, dipped his nose at a row of buttons and signs on Hecker's side of the glass: MEET MARC THE DOLPHIN. TALK TO HIM FOR 25¢. SPEAK INTO THE MIKE. HE UNDERSTANDS & WILL ANSWER YOU IN HIS COMPUTER-PRODUCED VOICE.

Hecker grinned back at the old dolphin. "Wait until I find some change."

"On the house," said the dolphin by way of a speaker grid next to the mike. He tapped out his messages on waterproof buttons inside his big tank. "I haven't had anyone to chat with in weeks. Not since my friend Jane was here last."

"Jane Kendry?"

"You know her?"

"I'm looking for her."

"She's here. A lot of them are here. But Jane hasn't been in to talk to me this trip. Too early probably, and there seems to be arguing going on. I'm patient. You learn that." He swam away from his computer buttons and looked long at Hecker through the glass. "You look trustworthy. So I can talk about Jane. A lot of people in this so-called republic are not to be trusted."

"How do you know Jane is here?"

"I'm still tuned in to parts of this place," explained Marc, back at his computer console. "Which is one reason why I stay on here. Another is, I'm used to it and I'm old. Why move back into the ocean at my age? Who knows what the ocean has gotten like. Everything changes, isn't that so?"

"I'd been noticing that," Hecker told the dolphin. "How do you keep alive?"

"Cleverness," said Marc. "I figured out ways to do things for myself, utilizing the computer and what's left of the communications, surveillance, and disposal systems here. Keeps me busy. The owner of Fish/Utopia!—isn't that a

138

vulgar name? The exclam at the end is particularly dreadful—the owner got out of business in something of a rush. One of the associate curators hung around, helped me fix this all up. At the time there wasn't much anyplace else I could go. Now I don't even care to move. You know, you get to thinking of someplace as your own turf. Home."

Hecker scratched his mustache, put one hand against the clear thick glass. "Can you tune in on what's going on around the campfires, Marc?"

"Sure can," assured the dolphin. "Marc is only my show-business name, by the way. Larry is my real name. Makes no difference actually. Who did you say you were?"

"James Xavier Hecker."

The dolphin swam back for another look at him. "Oh, so? Yes, they've been talking about you. Jane seems to be for you, but most of the others haven't a good word to say. Hold on a sec and I'll try to catch some of this."

"Good."

A crackling sound came, and then the loud roar of the sea. "No, that's the wrong pickup mike. That's in the fake lighthouse. Wait now. There you go."

"I am not either a cracker-headed ninny," came Rollo's voice. "How were we to know he was going to start a riot and hotfoot out? We figured even he'd have respect for Captain Nazi and sit still through the show. Giving you all plenty of time. After which we could beat him senseless and leave him in a gutter."

"Rollo was trying to pinch some chink girl," protested Milo. "Ask him if that didn't slow his already clodhopper wits. Didn't that dull your already clodhopper wits, you poor Mongolian idiot."

"Liking pretty Oriental teen-agers doesn't make you a

Mongolian idiot," said Rollo. "It's not catching, you rustic simp."

"Oof," grunted Milo.

"Stop this scuffling," ordered Jess Kendry, his voice harsh and fuzzy. "I'm tired of it. I think I'll go looking for this Hecker son of a bitch myself. This spy. Yes, and I won't just knock him senseless."

"Let it pass, Father," said Jane.

There was the sound of Jess slapping the girl. "I don't want any more of your smart talk, you hear? My wrath is aroused. Shut your mouth, Janey."

Marc the dolphin turned the eavesdropping pickup off. "That's been the general drift for quite a while. Milo and Rollo are new to the discourse, though."

"Must have just got back," said Hecker. "Where exactly are they?"

"That mike's in the Seal Arcade. Big old half-open theater about six blocks northeast of us here." He gestured with his snout.

"Thanks. We'll talk to you later."

"Perhaps you ought to run and hide. I have a hunch Jess Kendry wants to kill you."

"That," said Hecker, "is one of the things I want to talk over with him."

CHAPTER 18

Jess Kendry had a piano again. This was a white enameled upright with pastel mermaids and flying fish decorating it.

"He's a country boy, but the fool done come to town," Jess was singing. "Yes, he's a country boy, but the fool done come to town. He ain't doing nothing but tearing his poor self down."

Jess's left hand was thunking steady, but his righthand fingers were clumsy and stumbling and they hit the wrong keys and sometimes the spaces between.

About fifty guerrillas, all Kendrys, were sitting around in the old open-air theater. Most of the cook fires had been built in the clear area in front of the dry-seal pool, and Jess had his piano there too. Jane, her hands on her knees, sat directly behind him on one of the wood-and-stone benches.

"When he had money they called him Sweetie Pie," continued Jess. "Yes, when he had money they called him Sweetie Pie. But he's broke now and it's 'So long, country guy.'"

He attempted a walking bass and his two hands got tangled. He left off playing abruptly and spun on the white Neptune-decorated stool. "Lot of truth in that, Janey."

"Lot of bullshit too," she answered.

Rollo Kendry, slouching on a bench near her, said, "You hadn't ought to talk like that to close kin, Janey."

"Young people these days, especially young girls, lack a lot of respect," said Milo from his perch on the railing of the dead pool.

Hecker stopped watching and went straight down through the rows of seats, down the cement stairway that pointed at Jess and his piano. Hecker's lean, mustached face was calm, a slight grin resting on it. The flames of the guerrillas' fires gave him a flickering appearance.

Milo Kendry noticed Hecker first. "Great humping bull-pucky!"

"You don't talk so sweet yourself," began Rollo and then swung to catch sight of Hecker. "Hey, Jess, there he is."

Jess stood, lost his balance, sat on the piano keys with a rippling thump, fell back on the stool. "My wrath is strong," he shouted at Hecker. "Shame on you, shame. You've tried to betray us all."

Hecker moved nearer to Jane. She had half risen, one leg bent under her and still resting on the bench. "How are you?" they both said, quietly, at the same time. And then, "Fine."

"And my wrath is not to be messed with," said Jess. He made it to his feet and came toward Hecker.

Milo and Rollo, slightly hunched and arms free-swinging, were up and coming at him as well. Around the open-air theater others of the Kendry clan were rising, approaching.

"You're nothing but a sneaking Junta spy," roared Jess. "A child molester. Yes, a defiler of men's young daughters, who were raised as best I could after her mother was slaughtered in the street." He flung a pointed finger in the direction of Jane, then poked it in Hecker's face. "Shame, shame. What do you have to say for yourself?"

Hecker's tongue slid up under his upper lip for an instant, causing his shaggy mustache to rise and ripple. Then he said, "You took Jane. I'm here to see her."

"You're here to get your butt wiped," said Rollo. "You caused a mess for Captain Nazi and messed around with Jane and you're a spy for the Junta. We're now going to fix you good."

"No, you're not." Jane walked the few steps to Hecker's side.

"Get away from him," said Jess. "Your loyalty is to our cause, Jane. Our good work. Our mission is to free the Republic of Southern California from the yoke of Junta tyranny."

Jane shook her head. "No, it isn't. Not any more, not for a lot of you."

"You talk like the Junta," said Jess.

"I talk like myself," said Jane, "and you can't hear that." She put her hands, locked them, around Hecker's left arm. "No, this part is over. It's already happened and over. I'm not going to live on yesterday any more."

"Talk, talk," said Jess. "How does that help me live with the shame and grief you've caused me?"

"That's *your* problem," said Jane.

"Watch your mouth," said Rollo, sliding close to Jane.

143

Hecker pulled gently free of Jane and swung on Rollo. He connected with his chin, and Rollo, ringlets dancing, fell to the cement. "We'll go," Hecker told Jane.

Jess dashed up to them. "You'll have to knock me to the ground, too, before you can get out of here."

Hecker said, "We're leaving Jess Kendry. Just stop yourself."

Jane's father growled, squeezed both hands into fists, and swung them up and at Hecker's face. "You son of a bitch."

Hecker backed and the old man fell by, stumbled, hit the edge of a step with his knees.

Jane, for an instant, started to make a motion to help him up. She stopped. "No, it's all over."

Hecker took her hand and they walked up the stairway. The rest of the Kendrys gathered around the half-fallen Jess, looking from him to Hecker and Jane.

Jess's old hands fell open and stopped being fists. He raised one of them and shook it negatively at the angry clan. "No," he said, "let them go." He put the hand to his face and began to cry.

Blocks from there, at the town side of Fish/Utopia! Jane said, "I almost didn't."

"I know," said Hecker.

"Now it's better," she said. "Right. I won't go back. I won't pick him up any more." She inhaled deeply, laughing, crying.

A land truck rumbled up to the gates of the playland. "There was holes in the fuel tank but I fixed them all up," called Marsloff. "We decided to come looking for you. Here we are."

"Hi, Jane," said Jack from the seat next to Marsloff.

144

"Jack," said Jane. "Oh, good."

"You want a lift to Swingleton?" offered Marsloff.

Hecker said to the girl, "Want to keep on after Gadget Man?"

"Yes."

CHAPTER 19

The golden horse came loose from the spinning merry-go-round and shot across the purple-glass room, knocked over two gray-haired women in ruffled skirts. The calliope music stopped piping out of the dozen suspended silver outlets, and the merry-go-round slowed and halted finally.

A big round-shouldered young man in a loose coat-sweater, smoking a redwood pipe, flatfooted to the two knocked-over women. "Oh, nasty," he said. "What a nasty old thing to have happen. But just look here. Here's a nice stick of candy, made of purest soy by-products, for each of you. Yum yum."

"Stuff the candy," said the matron, who was still conscious. "You cold-cocked Beatrice with your slipshod horse. We moved into Swingleton to relax, not to be trampled."

"I know my horsey hurt you and your little pal," said

the man. "But you mustn't be mad at me. Don't be mad at Mr. Dappler. Because Mr. Dappler likes you. He loves you. He doesn't want you to be hurt."

"We'll slap a lawsuit on you, Dappler. And on old Swingle up in his tower. And on this dumb Kid Therapy Center. Then you can work your babytalk on the judge," said the gray-haired woman. She gripped the still-stunned Beatrice by the armpits and dragged her across the slick yellow floor and out into the misty afternoon sunshine.

Hecker shifted on the saddle of his unicorn and leaned toward Dappler. "We want to talk to you now."

"Hush, hush," he whispered, moving close to Hecker and Jane. "I don't know why I get involved in this illicit stuff at all. Be patient. I don't want you, as friends of Percher, to get mad. In a little minute I'll get to you." Dappler scratched his cleft chin with a stick of candy. Then he chuckled and clapped his hands. There were ten old people in the round room. "Well, now, let's all keep having a good time and pretend those bad girls were never here. They don't know how good acting out all one's childish feelings can be. They'll be sorry they made faces at the Swingleton Kid Therapy Center, won't they? We'll show them." He made a spinning motion with his head, and the merry-go-round jerked into motion.

Hecker got a new grip on the paper bag holding the small gadget Percher had given them. "Let's all be patient," he said to Jane.

A small gray man shuffled carefully along the moving floor of the merry-go-round and took the wooden lion between Hecker's unicorn and Jane's stallion. "See," he said to Hecker while his dust-colored lion rose and fell, "Dappler is a master of applying kid-psych theories. No musty cubicles of useless learning for him. He's the best therapist around. I was to three of them before I settled in Swingleton here. My first wife and I used to attend one in the Laguna Sector. A washout."

"Didn't help you?"

"Helped me, but not that bitch I was married to," said the frail old man. "She wouldn't use the kid therapy to relieve her adult problems. Instead, she'd throw the building blocks at me and pour sand down my front, and stuff little beads of modeling compound up my nose. You're not supposed, see, to do that. You're supposed to try very hard to recapture the lightness and fun of your childhood. The good stuff only. So you can cope with your senior problems."

"You get satisfaction with Dappler, though," said Hecker.

"He's been of considerable help to Tammy and myself," the old man said. "I lost my second wife, another bitch I might add, in a riot recently, and I was pretty gloomy. Then I met Tammy. She's only seventeen years old, and so she's much closer to the era of play and natural spontaneity." He lowered his voice. "She's a humdinger in bed, too."

The merry-go-round stopped again, and Dappler said, "Now the pretty ride is over and it's time for some real nice therapy. Out at the rings and slides."

"This next really lifts your worries off you," said the frail man, dismounting from his lion. "Want to race over there?"

"You take a headstart," Jane said.

Dappler slipped up to them, motioned for Hecker to let him see into the paper sack. He said, "Okay, don't even explain it to me. Those things make me feel creepy all over. It's bad enough here." From a lumpy pocket of his sweater he pulled out a plastic card. "This identifies you as visiting relatives. Go down the road here and turn left at the sandbox. Keep going till you come to the Club Repose. It's a hot spot for our senior citizens. Chef Joe Senco is buying for Swingle now. This pass'll get you to him with no trouble." He went running toward the door, tripped on a roller skate, fell. He glanced back at them and asked, "How's that little creepy Percher anyway? Never mind." He crawled outside on his hands and knees.

"What a way to make a living," Jane quoted.

They walked from the merry-go-round dome, following Dappler's directions. Everything was very clean in Swingleton, the tree-lined streets straight and wide, the fire hydrants chrome-plated.

An eighty-year-old man in a black cowboy suit stopped them on the clean vinyl grass path that led to the Club Repose's grilled door. "What's your blood type?"

Hecker showed him their pass. "This is all the identification we have."

"Listen, I'm Wally 'The Doctor' Flamm," explained the old man. There were buffalo heads on his neckerchief. "I attend lots of the old retired military coots here in Swingleton. Right now I'm getting ready for a rush transfusion on Rear Admiral Chatterton W. Gove, RSCN, Retired."

"He's sick, huh?"

"He's always sick," said Flamm. "Most of them *are* here. It's a bonanza for medical practice. Today the admiral is anemic, and I think I'll try Type O on him."

"Neither of us are O," Hecker told him. "But I hope you get his trouble cleared up."

"This anemia today is only one of his troubles," said Flamm. "Yesterday it was heart failure, and the day before a stroke. He keeps me hopping, the admiral does. He has great recuperative powers, though. Bounces back. 'Old Rubber Ball,' they used to call him. During the Brazilian

War, when he was attached to the United States Navy." Flamm sighed, removed his black sombrero. "Still, this isn't as bad as last week. Last week he had a thrombosis and went blind twice."

Jane asked, "You sure you're diagnosing him right, Doctor?"

"I'm not a doctor," said Flamm. "When I first introduced myself to you, if you recall, I was careful to label myself 'The Doctor.' In quotes."

"How come you practice medicine, then?" Hecker moved himself and Jane closer to the club.

"I had the call," said Flamm. "I, you know, just sensed it. I had a vision, you might say. This vision mentioned, among other things, I should be a doctor. So I immediately gave up a successful Potato Heaven route in Altadena, checked a bunch of medical books out of my local Junta Semi-Free Library, and went on from there."

"Good luck on Type O," said Jane.

"I'd settle for Type A," said Flamm, his boot heels and spurs clicking as he walked.

Chef Senco had six kettles going on the giant stove. "Gourmet cooking for people over eighty is a special kind of challenge," he told Hecker and Jane. "I've even tried to adapt some of the classic recipes of my idol Father Caparizzi, but it's a tough row to hoe."

"That smells good." Jane indicated the second kettle from the left.

"Oatmeal," sneered the plump chef. "Next to that, diced beets. Then creamed tuna and minced spinach." He paused and made a wincing motion. "That noise out there in the club proper keeps me in an emotional turmoil. I get little sharp pains all through here, and even way around here. They play shuffleboard and skittles day and night. Those are outdoor sports and should be undertaken in the sunlight." He trotted away from them, around his new butcher table. Reaching up, he thumped hanging copper pans with both small fists, making noises to counter those of the aged patrons of the Club Repose. "What did cute little Percher send in with you?"

From the paper sack Hecker took an electric weather house. "This gadget has the advantage of being practically an antique. One of those little houses where the witch comes out if there's going to be bad weather. Two little blond kids for fair weather."

"Cute," said Chef Senco. "What's the gimmick?"

"Notice the little figures," Hecker explained. "Each one has a tiny needle added now. The witch needle is drugs, and the blond kids are electric shock. You never know exactly which will pop out. This gadget combines the basic fun of Russian roulette with that of old-fashioned shock therapy. That's how Percher explains it. He wants a thousand dollars for this."

"I hope he gets over his flu," said Chef Senco. "It was flu you said?"

"Brazilian flu," said Jane.

"The worst kind." The chef pointed at them with a wooden spoon. "I tell you what. Percher has been so swell in thinking up ideas that old man Swingle wants to express his thanks in person. It's a real shame cute little Percher is laid up and didn't get in himself. Since old Swingle has this little appreciation ceremony in mind, we might as well go ahead with it. You two'll do as substitutes." He shuffled to the stove. "Let me turn the heat down low and I'll escort you to his tower suite."

"We're honored," said Hecker.

152

CHAPTER 20

The tower was higher than the one at the Rehab Center, and its smoky windows kept the sunlight almost completely out. Closed just inside the doorway, Jane said, "Not too good."

"That's what I thought when it turned out to be Second Lieutenant Same who opened the door," said Hecker.

Far across the room, behind a wide floor-standing beaded screen, Second Lieutenant Same was now talking to someone. At Hecker's and Jane's backs stood the chef, with a pistol resting against the string of his striped apron.

"He'd like to meet you," called Same, emerging from behind the screen. "You can get back to your kitchen, Joe."

The chef left, and Hecker and Jane approached the screen.

"We've been waiting to see what you'd do, Hecker. You haven't reported to the Social Wing since our encounter in the pavilion, where you did quite a lot of unnecessary damage, by the way. I had expected you'd try to get here by a more indirect means."

"I figured," said Hecker.

"Nevertheless, I took precautions to cover the possibility of your walking right in."

On the other side of the screen they met Erwin LeBeck Swingle. There was not much left of him. His head, his left arm, and his right leg to the knee. Everything else was chrome and vinyl, mechanical parts. He was wired and bolted. Cords and hoses trailed away from him and wound intricately across the smooth floor behind him. He was connected to an old computer that filled the rear wall, wired to a smaller console computer, which Second Lieutenant Same leaned against. Swingle was linked, too, with a complex pumping mechanism that made an endless seesaw noise just to the right of him.

"Gadget Man," spoke Jane softly.

"My continued life," said Swingle in a voice which didn't seem to be coming from his mouth, "is a miracle."

"Of sorts," said Hecker.

The old man's face was long, thin, infinitely wrinkled. "Transplants and spare parts have kept me alive. We entirely abandoned human replacements—when was it, Same?"

"Twenty years ago, sir."

"All machinery and gadgets now," Swingle told them. "Gadgets were always pleasure to me, and so I am pleased to be almost one myself. It's a miracle. Or have I mentioned that? Have I, Same?"

"Yes, sir."

"Two brains in addition to my own, to be on the safe side," said the very old man, "and I still slip up. Age, you

154

see. Age will try to trip you up no matter how slick and sly you are. I wager even when I am completely gadget I'll be forgetful. Still shake now and again. She's a pretty girl, isn't she, Same? So young and tall and straight."

"She has a bad posture, sir."

"On the contrary, Same, a lovely stance." The old man rubbed a metal part of himself with his one real hand and produced a grating sound. "We'll kill them both, I'm afraid. After you find out what they know and whom they've told." A bubble rose from the bottom to the top of the large tank of yellow fluid connected to the Gadget Man's major pumping apparatus.

"What," Hecker asked him, "are you actually up to?"

"He hasn't time to explain," put in Same.

"Oh, I do," corrected the old man. "I have time, Same. I'm ninety-four, young people, and nowhere near dying. My purposes, since you inquire, are quite simple. To overthrow the government of the Republic of Southern California. To return this part of the state to its rightful paths. Then we will also destroy the San Francisco Enclave. No hope of ever converting them back to traditional American values. Always was that way up there, even in the days when we had an America. Take over California. Have to destroy everyone in the Frisco Enclave. Don't call it Frisco, they used to say. I think I've put the plan well. I have three brains to think with. Same is leaning on one of them with that smug look on his face. No balls. No balls, but he works like the very devil. Like a gadget. We intend to rebuild America, young people. We'll eventually have the whole glorious country again. Not as it was in the dreadful nineteen-seventies and -eighties. Oh, no, as it was in an earlier day, a quieter day. I grew up in such a quiet place. There were almost five

155

acres of land, trees and fields. Late in the spring there would be wild flowers. Wild flowers all over, mind you. I knew the names of all of them. Butterflies, too. Dragonflies. They looked like biplanes. I suppose no one remembers biplanes now. They were from the First World War. Too many wars ago, I suppose. We fought a fellow named the Kaiser. Kaiser Bill, went around in a pointed hat. And my father—who has passed away, rest his soul—used to do all the chores and milk the cows by hand. No machinery for him. This was a long time ago."

Pumps, glass and metal, whirred and methodically ticked. "Why the riots?" Hecker asked the Gadget Man.

"To terrorize the Junta," said Swingle. "It is only part of my over-all plan. I am going to shift to more force soon, when things get to collapsing a bit more."

"How do you make the riots?" Jane asked.

Swingle laughed, inside himself someplace. "I use the Chinese."

"Which Chinese?" asked Hecker. "The Commandos?" He was still holding the weather house, and he tucked the bag up under his arm.

"Not plural, singular," said the old man. "As a matter of fact, though, he was a Commando. The Red Chinese were keeping him in reserve, but his unit got wiped out and never got to put him to use. We found him wandering, dazed and burned, in one of my orange groves. I learned what he could do, and I put him safe away until I was ready to use him. I'm immune to him. I made sure of that, too."

"What can he do?"

"He's a mass hypnotist," explained Swingle. "His name is Lee Bock, and we keep him locked up in the basement here."

"How do you use him?"

"We pick up a suburban community, rich and comfortable. Set up our television cameras, unobtrusively, and provide Lee Bock with assorted monitor pictures of the place. We also give him ordnance maps, chamber-of-commerce circulars, and other details about the suburb in question. Then Lee Bock concentrates and concentrates and wills the people to riot." The old man laughed again. "He's a mystic. He didn't even want to be a Commando. They conscripted him from his hometown in Tibet. If he doesn't do what we tell him, we don't feed him. Same is immune to Lee Bock, one of the reasons I let him work for me, and he has ways of persuading Lee Bock to make riots for us."

"This Lee Bock is right here in the basement?" asked Jane.

"Yes, indeed," replied the Gadget Man.

"Curious," said Hecker. He rocked forward and overhanded the packaged weather house into the open glass tank of Swingle's biggest pump. The witch figure fell free and bounced out of the tank and into the wires and circuitry next to it.

Hollow thunking bubbles began to form in the tank, and parts of the pump started buzzing and creaking. "Not them," gasped Swingle, waving Second Lieutenant Same's rising pistol down. "Attend to me first."

"But, sir."

Hecker took Jane's hand and they ran around to the other side of the screen. They stopped and pushed, flat-handed, until the big screen began to teeter and rock. One final grunting shove, and they got the screen to topple over onto Same and Swingle.

157

"Downstairs," said Hecker.

Beneath the beaded screen were sounds of breaking and sputtering, fizzling and splashing, offkey whirs and running-down grates.

CHAPTER 21

The basement was confused. The lighting, overhead tubes and strips meant to glow pale orange, was flickering and going off. Doors were opening and closing on their own, swishing and clicking. Door chimes were bonging in hundreds of rooms throughout the tower.

Three attendants in pale-lemon smocks ran by Hecker and Jane and up a ramp. "A government raid," panted one of them. "It must be."

A door slid open at the moment Hecker passed it. In the low, shadowy room sat an old Chinese man in a white bathrobe with no belt. "You are Hecker," said the Chinese, a tall man with a faint bend to him.

"Yes. You're Lee Bock?"

"I am," he said. "I foresaw your arrival and have been awaiting you. All this building's mechanisms are connected with Swingle himself. Another egocentric touch of his. Your monkey-wrenching has botched the entire structure, and it will no longer function well. How do you do, Jane Kendry."

"Pretty good. Yourself?"

"Weary," replied Lee Bock. He left the scuffed leather armchair he'd been sitting in and picked a small towel-tied bundle from the matted floor. "We can leave now." As they began hurrying up a ramp toward the outside, he added, "I must warn you, Hecker, of what I have foreseen. You should not return to your profession. You can not, I am afraid, trust even your superiors in the Social Wing." He kept up with Hecker, running as fast. "Manipulation Council has long controlled the Police Corps and its Social Wing. Though you did not know this, you work for them."

"No," said Hecker.

"You don't believe me?"

"Sure, I believe you. I meant I didn't work for anybody now. I meant I'm on my own. Most of what you just told me I've figured out while we've been on this Gadget Man quest."

"This is very good to hear," said Lee Bock, resting one smooth, ancient hand on Hecker's arm. "You will not return. You will not deliver Jane Kendry to anyone."

"I'm staying with Jane. Outside someplace."

"Oh?" said Jane. "That's very good to hear, too."

"Sometimes," said the Chinese mystic at the end of the ramp, "we do not need special perception to see and understand what is to be seen and understood."

The lane they'd reached was flanked with artificial orange trees in blossom. "They'll come after us before we can clear the outskirts of Swingleton," said Hecker.

"I have thought about that," said Lee Bock. His robe ballooned, and his paisley shorts flashed for an instant.

"As a diversion, Hecker and Jane Kendry, I will cause a riot. My last insurrection." He halted them beneath an orange tree. "Stand close to me, rest your hands on my shoulders so you won't run the risk of being affected by the impulses I will create." They did, and Lee Bock closed his eyes and gripped his elbows. A full minute went by. "We can proceed," said the Chinese mystic. "There should soon be sufficient diversions."

From the dental clinic on their right came a shatter of glass and then thousands of tooth X-rays fluttered out of an upper window. At the golf course next to the clinic a foursome of knickered old men began chasing a grounds-keeper with their irons. Old women were abandoning their patios, starting to conspire in larger and larger groups beneath rustic lampposts.

They began to run in a direction opposite to that of the growing crowds. "Do you get the whole population usually?" Hecker asked.

"No," said Lee Bock. "Only those who are really dissatisfied already."

Hecker took Jane's hand. They left the town as fires began to burn.

161